"This is wh[...] the young Lieutenant yelled.

"End of the line," he added with a little smile. Harmon Rabb knew that smile, at any given moment you could see it on the faces of personnel in any branch of the service—it said: "better you than me, pal."

Harm smiled back weakly and then looked over at the flight engineer who was standing at the edge of the open hatch, preparing the winch and delivery sling it would lower. The sling looked awfully small and the winch looked a little worn, as if it was not in tip-top working order.

"I'm getting in that?" Rabb yelled, pointing at the sling.

"Yes sir," the Lieutenant shouted back.

Now Harm pointed down at the huge submarine righting itself on the surface of the roiling water. "I'm getting in that to go down there?"

The co-pilot nodded vigorously. "That's the plan, sir."

Harm shrugged and shook his head slowly. This, he thought, was one *hell* of a way to practice law.

JAG

The Novel

ROBERT TINE

BERKLEY BOULEVARD BOOKS, NEW YORK

JAG: THE NOVEL

A Berkley Boulevard Book / published by arrangement with
Paramount Pictures Corporation

PRINTING HISTORY
Berkley Boulevard edition / March 1998

The Putnam Berkley World Wide Web site address is
http://www.berkley.com

ISBN: 0-425-16485-3

BERKLEY BOULEVARD
Berkley Boulevard Books are published by The Berkley Publishing Group,
a member of Penguin Putnam Inc.,
200 Madison Avenue, New York, New York 10016.
BERKLEY BOULEVARD and its logo are trademarks
belonging to Berkley Publishing Corporation.

PRINTED IN THE UNITED STATES OF AMERICA

10 9 8 7 6 5 4 3 2 1

JAG

The Novel

prologue

DURING THE NIGHT, A "BERMUDA DOME" had moved in from the Atlantic, changing the temperature in southern Virginia and the North Carolina border from pleasant fall weather, temporarily pushing the area back into summer. Temperatures went up to well above the eighty degree mark and the air was hot and sticky, and scarcely stirred by the light winds. The early Thanksgiving decorations in store windows looked out of place as Tom Turkeys and paper Puritans wilted in the heat.

But there was a certain festivity in the sticky air. A substantial part of the U.S. Navy Atlantic Fleet was in Newport News. There were two big carriers, the USS *Eisenhower* and the USS *Independence*, several Aegis carriers, along with a gaggle of destroyers and missile frigates. Also in port were two huge Trident submarines, vast, blunt-nosed black vessels that looked out of place on the surface.

All of these ships had disgorged thousands of sailors into the streets, filling the bars and restaurants—all of them looking for relaxation, sin, adventure, or even a mixture of all three. The sailors were everywhere, thronging the streets, idling on street corners, cursing the heat and the Navy (as usual) on the lookout for the Shore Patrol, officers, or women.

There were five high-ranking officers that the average sailor did not have to worry about running into. A few miles away from the bustling streets of the port, an elegant yacht, the Cats Paw II, nosed through the calm waters of lower Chesapeake Bay, the passengers five prominent officers of the United States Navy. The five were dressed in civilian clothes and were seated around a teak table in the fantail, cocktails being served by discreet, faultlessly efficient Navy mess stewards.

Conversation was casual, low-key, humorous—with some gentle ribbing thrown in—the kind of meandering, easy talk that one is likely to find among a group of old, old friends.

One of the men sipped his martini, looked into the darkening sky, and swallowed. ''Tell me, Eric, is this old tub yours? Or is it *ours*?''

There was something about Eric McKitrick that marked him as the host of this particular gathering. It was he who had welcomed the other four aboard, it was into his ear that the Chief Steward whispered when he had a question about when to serve the hors d'ouevres or which wines to decant with dinner. Of the five, as rear Admiral, he held the highest rank.

"This old tub, Will, is an asset of the United States Navy, paid for and maintained by the ever-munificent bounty of the great United States taxpayer."

A third man held up his scotch and soda and toasted. "God bless 'em," he said, his words slightly slurred.

Captain Joseph Phillips was usually the first of the group to get drunk. Of course, they would all be more or less in the bag by the time the evening had come to an end. All, of course, except for Marine Colonel Steven Conroy. He would drink as much—maybe more—than any of the others, but by midnight he would still look as if he was ready to make his formation, like a good square Marine.

"And in the event of war?" asked one of the men. "What happens to this old tub then, Eric?"

Admiral McKitrick laughed and sipped his drink, a vial of Belvedere vodka chilled to the point of being almost as viscous as motor oil. "Then she puts to sea and engages the enemy, Allen."

The last of the five spoke. "Bombarding the enemy with volley after volley of champagne corks, right?" said Allen Hawkes, laughing. He too drank vodka.

"Why do I have a feeling that she'll steam up the Potomac," said Phillips, "load on a couple of senators who'll get bombarded with champagne, wined and dined without mercy or favor until they strike their colors, and they've agreed to give you more money for that Goddamn spook palace you run?"

Eric laughed heartily. "You know the service, Joe. They send you where they need you."

Of course, "this old tub" was nothing of the sort. Rather, it was an eighty-six-foot Martinolich fantail motor yacht, a long, white, stately craft, whose keel had been laid a long time ago, in 1924. McKitrick had acquired the vessel as a hulk somewhere on the West Coast and meticulously restored it—payment coming from the vast "black" budget Admiral McKitrick oversaw as head of the deeply secret NCIS—Naval Combat Intelligence Systems. The other four men were "hands-on" Navy—three of them were commanders of considerable Naval vessels—but McKitrick was a spy, more at home in the trench warfare of the Pentagon and Capitol Hill than in actual armed conflict. No less demanding, perhaps—but a lot safer. He had served on fighting vessels, of course, but those days were gone for good. Admiral McKitrick did not regret that the M/Y Cats Paw was as close as he would ever come to another floating command.

These five men dined together once a year and they had done so every year since they had graduated from the U.S. Naval Academy in the summer of 1967. They had gone through Annapolis together and then made their way in the service, climbing the steep slope toward the various peaks of the Navy.

Of course, reunions of the five members of the Davey Jones Locker Club had not always been as elaborate as this one. The very first reunion, in 1968, had taken place in the back room of a decidedly sleazy bar near the huge Naval base in San Diego, a joint called Pete's, that crawled with drunk sailors and sharp-eyed hookers. No one could remember what they ate that night, but nobody could forget the drink—a lethal concoction called "Anchor Grease." It was made of several parts vodka, tequila, and gin, and made drinkable by a pitcher of sweet pink lemonade—overall, it was *all* parts poison. Not one of them would ever forget the hangover . . .

The five had been good, God-fearing middies at Annapolis, all of them, like the rest of the class, taking a long, hard look at the possibility of service in the Republic of South Vietnam. They had not been the athletic stars or the great brains of their class, but they had been well-liked by their superiors and their fellow classmen; they had acquired mentors and protectors who would watch over their subsequent careers. No one, though, would have predicted that this group in particular, would have traveled so far so fast.

Rear Admiral Eric McKitrick was the highest-ranking and most powerful of the group, in political terms, anyway. The others wielded other, more blunt, types of power.

Captain Will Mattingly commanded the USS *Tennessee,* one of the big nuclear-powered Trident submarines docked across the bay. Contained in that black tube was more destructive power than had been unleashed in all the wars ever fought. Yet Mattingly was an unprepossessing man, small, rather scrawny, a shock of white hair on his head, with a curiously friendly cast to his blue eyes.

Marine Colonel Steve Conroy was the only member of the group who had not arrived on a ship. Rather, he had helo'd in from Fort Bragg, flying himself in Bell OH-58D Kiowa Warrior helicopter, a needle-snouted helicopter armed with Hellfire anti-tank missiles, Stinger air-to-air missiles, Hydra 70 rockets, and a brace of 12.75 machine guns, as if he expected real trouble somewhere in the treacherous airspace over North Carolina. Conroy was a SEAL, and he looked the part. He was compact and wiry, but there was obvious strength and power in his large hands and hard shoulders and forearms. Rock-jawed and buzz-cut, he looked as if no matter what he wore, he was always, in his mind, dressed in full camouflage.

By contrast, Captain Allen Hawkes looked buttoned-down and low-profile, and he wore his casual clothes like a businessman who had just stepped off the golf course. He had arrived at Newport in the grandest style possible: driving the USS *Eisenhower*, one of the Navy's newest and most powerful supercarriers. Nearly a quarter-mile long, with a crew of five thousand and compliment of 250 airplanes, Captain Hawkes commanded more firepower in that single vessel than the majority of most of the countries of the world.

The fifth man was Captain Joseph Phillips and there was no doubt that his entrance had been the most humble. He was no less a sailor, no less capable than the others, but the U.S. Navy had, in its wisdom, seen fit to put him in charge of the USS *Mackinac*. The "Mac" was not, like the "Ike", a supercarrier, neither was it a powerful submarine like the *Tennessee*.

The Mackinac was a supply ship, an enormous one—
bigger than a battleship and almost as fast—but it was
a supply ship nonetheless. Civilians—even the uni-
formed in the Navy—would have thought that somehow, Captain Joe had not done quite as well as his
Annapolis classmates. They would be wrong about
that.

Actually, being entrusted with the command of
such a huge vessel was a vote of confidence and was
well-known as the last stop before being given the
helm of an aircraft carrier. Being able to demonstrate
facility of command on a behemoth like the Mackinac
was ample proof that the Captain deserved one of the
prized fourteen carriers in the U.S. fleet.

Still, the Mackinac was not the transport Phillips
would like to have been driving. Like any other
supply-ship commander, he wanted a carrier, but all
fourteen were captained by men in the prime of their
careers. It seemed unlikely that there would be a va-
cancy any time soon, and Captain Joe's career was
now in its twilight years. He did not want to end his
service at the command of the Mackinac, and he was
not afraid to say so.

Over a dinner of smoked salmon, duck, and braised
leeks, Phillips helped himself to another glass of a
superb Bordeaux, sipped it, and smirked at Hawkes.
"How are you feeling, Al? Any little aches and
pains? Feeling the weight of your age? Wouldn't you
like to put down that heavy burden of command?"

Hawkes and the rest of the diners were used to this
line of questioning. It had been going on ever

since Phillips had taken over command of the *Mackinac*.

"Feeling great, Joe. Never felt better. In fact, I'm thinking of petitioning the Joint Chiefs for an extended career."

"That's great, Al," said Joe Phillips, his face showing mock eagerness. "That's the idea. The next step up off the Ike is the Pentagon. You could go work with Eric—reading other people's mail."

Hawkes laughed. "Oh, hell, Joe—you know I'd only extend my hitch *if* they promised to leave me on the *Eisenhower*."

Phillips pounded the table so hard the cutlery rattled, and for a moment it looked to the others as if he were genuinely angry. "Goddamit, Al! Why don't you let someone else have a turn? I'm sick of driving that glorified tractor trailer all over the map. . . ." Then Phillips smiled. "How about the other thirteen carrier jocks," he said. "I know you're all in a secret society or something—any of them feeling their age?"

"Well . . . I hear that Charlie Honnegger on the *Lexington* is just about at death's door."

Phillips raised his glass. "Gentlemen, to the ill health of Captain Charlie Honnegger!"

There was laughter from around the table. Charlie Honnegger, who had been a year ahead of them all at Annapolis, was a great bull of a man who had played tackle for the Mids in one of their rare winning seasons. The chances were good that he would live to see all five people at the table into their graves, and then live to be ninety-nine at the very least.

Dessert was served with after-dinner drinks—but not the expensive cognacs and other cordials one might have expected from such a well-heeled host on board such a graceful vessel. Instead, a steward placed a large crystal punch bowl in the middle of the table—the pale pink color left no doubt as to the make of the potion. It was Anchor Grease . . .

By eleven that night, all were drunk. By midnight, they were singing songs of such graphic obscenity that it was just as well they were far out at sea. At that point, no tighter group of friends could be found.

Or so it seemed.

one ✈

"WEEKEND WARRIORS" WAS BASED AT AN isolated old airfield, deep in rural Virginia, the few dilapidated hangars housing a historical timeline of aircraft that were available for charter, if you could produce the right licenses and certification. If not, one of the pilots that actually ran the place would take you up for a ride in the plane of your choice. All this for a fee, of course.

The planes in the hangars were a museum of flying history. There were a number of old but well-maintained biplanes, like an old Curtiss JN–4D Jenny for anyone interested in reliving the golden age of barnstorming, along with a couple of World War One-era Spads and an English Sopwith Camel.

The aircraft of the Second World War were well-represented as well, but only with aircraft from the Allied side of the war. This was not due to any prejudice on the part of the management—an old aviator named Spike Kelleher, who had managed to fly in every armed conflict the U.S. had been involved in since the late days of World War Two to the early days of Vietnam—but because the destruction of the Luftwaffe had been so complete that very few classic machines from that era still existed. Still, you could refight the Battle of Britain in a Hurricane or a Spitfire, or pretend to duel with Mitsubishi Zeroes in a P–51 Mustang. There was even a rare Grumman F7F Tigercat still dressed in her Marine markings and paint, a sight to stir the heart of any old Leatherneck flier.

For weeks now, Lieutenant Commander Harmon Rabb had been promising himself that he would get out to the field and sign himself up for some airtime in one of the old classics, but somehow he had never gotten around to it. However, when he heard that Spike had acquired a new plane, the jewel of his collection, he immediately found time to get out there.

For years Kelleher had been negotiating with the Republic of the Ukraine to buy an old MiG—an MiG 15, to be exact. Kelleher had done most of his combat flying in Korea, and the MiG 15 had been his nemesis. Back in the 1950's the blunt-nosed single-seat MiG had been better than just about anything the United Nations forces had been able to put into the sky. The legendary aircraft was the aerial equivalent of the Kalashnikov assault weapon: simple, hardy, and deadly as hell. The small, slightly bulbous machine was not pretty, but it could fly at a top speed of over six hundred miles per hour, had a range of well over twelve hundred miles, and could drop a ton of bombs on you before you heard it coming. Many an American flier had been shot down under the murderous rate of fire in two 23mm cannons carried in the wings.

Spike Kelleher wanted one the way he wanted a girl he could never get. It cost him a hundred thousand dollars, but he figured it was worth it. Harmon Rabb couldn't help but agree.

The MiG stood on the hardstand in front of its hangar, the silver paint gleaming dully in the morning air. It looked tense on its slim undercarriage, as if ready to leap into the air.

Rabb was already in his flight suit, waiting while the chase plane took off and got into position circling the airfield. Mounted in the nose of the chase plane—a lowly Beechcraft—was a cluster of cameras aimed like machine guns. Part of the service at Weekend Warriors was a nice set of pictures you could put on your mantel, showing you at the controls of the aircraft of your choice. In the case of the MiG 15, you got takeoff and landing pictures only because once the jet was airborne and the afterburner kicked in could the Beech hope to keep up.

"It's not exactly pretty is it, Spike?" Rabb asked Kelleher as the two men gazed at the plane.

The old airman shook his head. "Nope. And it gets worse. When you see it coming out of the sun at you, those Goddamn cannons going, it's not only not pretty, it's the most terrifying thing you've ever seen. Flies like the devil, though. It's a wonder we ever shot any down in face-to-face aerial combat.'' Kelleher sighed heavily and Harm could see that the old man was thinking of those fliers who never came back after a tangle with an MiG 15.

"I tried for three years to get it here and when they finally unloaded it I couldn't look at it.'' Kelleher jammed his hands into his faded khakis. "Then once I looked at it, I wanted to take a fire axe to it . . .''

"Then?''

"Then . . . I flew it.'' The old man smiled and pushed Harm toward the MiG, as if trying to get him to ask a girl to dance. "Don't break it.''

Harm squeezed into the tight, spartan cockpit of the MiG. The Russians had never believed in coddling their pilots—the seat was hard, the cockpit was tight, the instruments were basic.

"No bells and whistles on this baby . . .'' Harm whispered as the canopy was slid shut over his head. It was plain that the MiG was a fast, maneuverable platform with a power pack of firepower. How it was used was up to the skill of the pilot.

The noise of the engine was overwhelming—it was mounted right under the cockpit and Harm was virtually sitting on it, feeling the vibration of the fans in every bone of his body—but beyond that he felt the tingle of excitement, the kind of elation that fliers can never quite explain to the earthbound.

He was concentrating so hard, he did not notice

the nondescript beige Chrysler with markings from the Falls Church motor pool coming to a screeching halt in front of the clubhouse next to the MiG hangar. The plane eased forward smoothly, traveling across the tarmac toward the single long runway of the airfield.

Harm turned the MiG at the top of the strip and pointed the nose down the straight black strip. There was no other view as exciting as that one—except, perhaps, the landing strip on a carrier that heaved and rocked on a rough sea. But that was not a view Harm would ever see again.

"Departure, this is MiG 15, requesting clearance."

There was an unnervingly long silence, then Spike Kelleher's voice filled his head. "Hold on a minute there, Harm."

"There a problem, Spike?"

A moment later Bud Roberts's voice crackled in his headset. "Sir? Thank God, I got here before you took off."

"Bud? What the hell do you want?" Harmon Rabb may not have known what the young Lieutenant wanted, but he was sure that he was not going to be flying an MiG that fine, sunny morning.

"Admiral Chegwidden wants to see you, sir." Harm could tell that Bud Roberts hated being the bearer of bad news. "And he wants to see you immediately. As in right now, sir."

"What's this all about, Bud?"

"Sorry, sir. I can't tell you."

"Why not?"

"Because it's level seven security, sir. . . ."

Harmon Rabb felt a jolt that had nothing to do with the MiG. "Roger that, Bud," he said and began to turn the MiG around, taxiing back to the hangar. Security level seven's didn't come along that often. When Harm had left word of his whereabouts with the JAG offices that morning all had been quiet. Now, it seemed, something had blown up big time.

two ✈

BUD ROBERTS DROVE AS FAST AS HE
dared back across northern Virginia, delivering Lieutenant Commander Rabb to the JAG headquarters at Falls Church just forty-five minutes after climbing out of the cockpit of the MiG.

The military never really shut down—Saturday was just another workday in the offices of the Judge Advocate General—and things were a lot busier now at mid-morning than when Harmon Rabb had checked in just before dawn. Every elevator was full and there were lines waiting to get on them. Harm hit the stairs, climbing four flights in thirty seconds. Not bad. . . .

The waiting room to Admiral Chegwidden's office was crowded with men and women looking for a moment of the great man's time. He nodded hello to a couple of the JAG lawyers waiting there with stacks of briefs piled on their laps, and slid into a seat. Harm assumed he would have to take his place in line, but no sooner had his ass touched the seat, then the intercom on the secretary's desk buzzed.

"Is Lieutenant Commander Rabb here yet?" Chegwidden asked. He did not sound happy at having been kept waiting. The other lawyers in the room looked at Rabb with something like pity in their eyes.

"He just came in, sir."

"Good. Send him in."

Harm shot the secretary a friendly "thanks for nothing" look and then slipped into Chegwidden's office. The Admiral, sitting behind his huge desk, had that grim look in his blue eyes, a look Harm had seen far too frequently during his career at JAG. Chegwidden was deeply tanned and his hair was close-cropped; the most prominent feature was his ears, which were large and stood out from the sides of his shaved head. No one had mentioned the size of the Admiral's ears (to his face that is) since his days at the academy.

"What the hell is 'Weekend Warriors?'" Chegwidden growled. "You don't get enough action around here on weekdays? You better not be out with a bunch of jackasses shooting paint at each other." Chegwidden had been a SEAL in Vietnam. There was no such thing as a "war game" in his lexicon. He had seen too much to ever consider war something you played at.

"It's a collection of vintage aircraft, sir," said Harm. "Available to qualified fliers. I was about to take off in an MiG 15 when I got your call to come in. And I'm sorry I'm late, sir."

Chegwidden grunted and waved off the apology. He knew that Harmon Rabb had Navy flying in his blood, only a night-vision problem had washed him out of flying jets. Secretly, Admiral A. J. Chegwidden was pleased and proud that Rabb had decided to stay in the Service and go through all the trouble to qualify for JAG. Though it would have taken torture in the extreme to get him to admit it.

"Sit down."

Harmon Rabb sat. The Admiral did not look happy—but neither did he look angry. Rather, to Rabb's immense surprise, he realized that his superior looked sad—deeply sad.

"The reason I called you here," he began. "Is that . . ." But then his voice trailed off. The Old Man turned and looked out past his fleet of glass-encased model ships, and through the window beyond. It took him several seconds to regain whatever it was he had lost.

"I called you here," he began again, "because we had a very serious incident happen last night. A 'mysterious' death is what they are calling it. I need someone to look into it for me."

Harm had slipped a small, leather-bound notebook out of the inside pocket of his jacket and uncapped his pen, ready to take notes.

Chegwidden looked up and glared at the pad and pen as if Rabb had pulled a gun on him. "For God's sake, Rabb!" he bellowed. The sadness was gone, replaced by the crusty old Admiral that Harmon Rabb knew so well.

"Put those damn things away! There will be no notes, no transcripts, nothing on paper," Chegwidden growled. "Do I make myself clear?"

"Yes, sir," said Rabb crisply. He shut the notebook and put it in his pocket. But he was unnerved by this order of the Admiral's. Anything not on paper meant trouble, *big* trouble. And with no paper trail to protect himself if Harm found himself in this trouble over his head.

"This 'mysterious death' is being investigated by NIS," said Chegwidden. "As you know, it has already been classified level seven, so only a handful of people know about it now. How long that'll last . . ." Chegwidden shrugged, suggesting that the security lockdown would not last long at all. "I want you to get into it, quick. Before the circus starts, because there *is* going to be one."

"Yes, sir." Rabb was nodding agreeably, as if he understood exactly what his superior officer was talking about, but inside it was as if he could feel the quicksand beginning to pool around his feet. The Old Man was being uncharacteristically vague, as if he didn't even want to share information with one of his own operatives. That was a very bad sign.

"May I ask, sir, whose death we are talking about?" he asked diffidently. "I mean, who is the deceased?"

The Admiral looked up at him sharply. "Allen Hawkes," he said, brusquely. "An old friend of mine."

Harm almost jumped when he heard the name. This was just as gruesome as he had feared it would be. *Damn,* he thought. *I don't want any part of this.* The quicksand was up around his ankles, now.

"Al and I were in Vietnam together," said Chegwidden, his voice low. "He was driving Riverine boats back then. We used them for infiltration, and he was the best. He could squeeze one of those boats in Charlie's back pocket so he wouldn't notice. He was a great guy. Family man. Dedicated. A loyal American. Saltwater in his veins." For an embarrassing moment, Chegwidden's eyes glistened and he looked away from Rabb.

It was a nice obituary, Rabb thought, but it didn't tell the whole story. One of the elite fourteen had died under mysterious circumstances. Harm was nothing less than stunned.

"What happened, sir?" he heard himself asking.

Chegwidden got up from behind the desk and looked out the window. "They found his body in Officer Billet Row in Newport." He spoke slowly, as if he could not quite believe what he was saying. "Two bullets in the heart. No one heard anything. No one saw anything."

"He was murdered?" Harm blurted out.

The Old Man swung around and glared at Harmon Rabb, and their eyes locked. "Go find out why and who."

"Yes, sir."

"And Rabb . . ."

"Sir?"

"Find out fast."

A few minutes later, Harmon Rabb stumbled back into his own office in the JAG building. He was sweating. Why did it have to be so damn hot—it was October, after all.

He sat behind his own desk and snapped open the briefcase, removing the five dossiers Chegwidden had given him, placing them carefully on the desktop, as if they were unexploded bombs. In a sense, they were—they were the five service folders of the dead man and the last four men to see him alive, the members of the Davy Jones Locker Club. Lieutenant Commanders in the JAG corps were not usually privy to such sensitive documents—any one of these men, except for Hawkes, of course—could end up CNO or on the Joint Chiefs, and if they had any secrets, Harmon Rabb did not want to know them. He eyed the piles of paper suspiciously, as if he were afraid that one of them—or all of them—would start ticking like a bomb.

But these were the keys to the strange case that had just fallen into his lap, and he would have to read them all—probably memorize them—before this investigation was done. Then he would do his best to get a great case of amnesia. . . . He reached for the first of the folders just as the door of his office opened.

Mac walked in. "What are you doing here? I thought you had signed out for the weekend."

She was dressed in civvies and had an overnight bag slung over one shoulder, and looked as beautiful as ever. Behind her back, she was known as the best-looking Marine in the whole Corps. Rabb privately agreed with this assessment.

"I got signed in again," Rabb said. "I suddenly became very busy. Close the door, would you?"

But before she could, a seaman appeared in the doorway staggering and sweating under the weight of three large gunnysacks.

"Delivery for Lieutenant Commander Rabb," the sailor managed to pant. "Any place I can set these down, sir?"

"What are they?" Rabb asked.

"I don't know, sir. Admiral's orders. I just deliver them."

"Put 'em in the corner."

The sailor dumped his burden, saluted, and made quickly for the door, relieved that his job was done.

Harm put down the first folder and walked over to the pile of sacks. "What's all this?"

"I assume it's not your dirty laundry," Mac said with a little smirk.

Harm studied the three bags, frowned, and then turned to Mac. "Look at the address tags."

"Naval Special Weapons and Tactics Training Center," she read aloud. She looked at Harm, puzzled and shaking her head slightly. "That's spook school, isn't it, Harm?"

Rabb nodded. "That's right."

"Who do you know there?"

"No one," Harm replied. "That's the problem. . . ." He broke the seal on the first bag and pulled out the contents. There was a pair of heavy combat utilities along with a heavy flak jacket, boots, helmets, goggles, and a separate bag of heavy weather gear. All of it was conspicuously marked: Waterproof.

Harm felt his heart sink. The quicksand was up around his knees now.

"That's some addition to your wardrobe, Harm," said Mac, laughing a little. "What's it for?"

"It's for getting very wet," Harm replied, staring at her. "In very rough seas. That's what it's for."

At that moment, the phone on Rabb's desk rang. Mac grabbed it. "JAG, Commander Rabb's office . . ." Mac listened for a moment, making quick notes on a legal pad on the desk.

"Okay," she said and hung up. She turned to Harm, looking a little shocked and sort of amused at the same time.

"That was your travel agent," she said. "They want you to get dressed in this stuff. You're to meet a SH-53 helicopter at Andrews at 1600 hours. They said you should be prepared to be airborne for a very long time."

"That's a joke, right?"

"I don't think so, Harm." She picked up the phone and made as if to hand it to him. "But if you want to call them back . . ."

Harm looked down at the waterproof gear and shuddered. A few moments before, he had been complaining about the heat. Now he knew he was bound for somewhere very cold and very wet.

24

three ✈

NOBODY LIKED THE CH-53 HELICOPTER known as the Sea Stallion—not the Marines who generally flew them, nor anybody in any branch of the service who had to ride in them. The one that Harm Rabb was traveling in had been circling for over three hours now, the enormous flying beast going around and around the same patch of rough, gray ocean.

Harm had seen Sea Stallions before, even ridden in them, but he never really got used to them. There was something ungainly and clumsy about them. They were too big, too heavy, too loud—too complicated a contraption to actually get off the ground. Stories about these crapcans were legendary. Some exploded.

25

Some took off and then returned to the ground almost immediately. Some took off, snored away through the sky, and were never heard from again. The problem with the Sea Stallions was that these craft were called upon to do tough, dangerous jobs—a hundred hours flight time on the CH-53 engines was like a thousand on a Bell 430 or AH-1W.

The Sea Stallions were Navy craft, rugged, durable, two enormous engines running at all times. Their primary task was operating from aircraft carriers to land bases, ferrying emergency supplies and personnel back and forth. What that meant was the Sea Stallions spent a lot of time over water, running into sudden ocean storms that banged and buffeted the craft, hammering them to the edge of endurance.

Harmon Rabb was clad in all the rough weather gear that had come from the Naval Special Weapons and Tactics Training Center, wearing what felt like hundreds of pounds of rubber, leather, nylon and felt, but he was not assured by the tons of clothing. He was strapped into the hold of the flying monster—and this Sea Stallion seemed especially loud, big, and unstable. And now night was falling . . . and he didn't see too well at night.

They had reached the rendezvous point a few hundred miles off the Maryland coast, just as the sun was sinking under the horizon and, as soon as the pilot turned on his running lights, Harm began to feel the cold, despite all of his gear. That morning he had been complaining about the heat; now he was downright chilly. And he was doing three things he really hated to do: flying in a shaky helicopter at night over water.

"Or is that four things?" he asked aloud. But his voice was puny against the roar of the two big engines and the constant, earsplitting threshing of the huge rotors.

Of course, it didn't help that he still had no idea where he was going or why he was flying around and around way the hell out here in the middle of nowhere. The pilots and crew didn't know either—not that they had expected to be filled in on anything. They had their orders: get to a certain point on the map at a certain time and wait. And they were doing their job very well, Harm thought. Damn them.

As they circled for another thirty minutes or so, the air outside the behemoth grew more turbulent, as if it had a mind of its own and had decided to make things a little more unpleasant for Lieutenant Commander Harmon Rabb. A few minutes earlier, the flight engineer had sent a message forward to the flight crew. Harm was sure it was a report on a weather change, and that was *not* good.

But then he saw the copilot climbing out of his seat and crawling back in his direction.

"You ready, sir?" The copilot, a Lieutenant, had yelled right into Harm's ear, but he could barely hear him.

"Ready?" Harm bellowed back. "Ready for what?"

The Lieutenant did not reply. He pointed to a crewman who was opening a hatch window, and then indicated that Harm should look down.

Harm looked. There was nothing but black water down there. Black, angry water flecked with whitecaps, and it seemed to be miles down. Then, before Harm's eyes, the ocean seemed to rise up, bubbling as if it were boiling up, as if it were going to engulf the chopper. The white waves parted to reveal something very dark, wet, and sinister. Something enormous.

It was a huge Trident submarine, the wide blunt prow breaking the surface directly below the Sea Stallion.

"This is where we hand you off, sir," the young Lieutenant yelled. "End of the line," he added with a little smile. Harmon Rabb knew that smile, at any given moment you could see it on the faces of personnel in any branch of the service—it said "better you than me, pal."

Harm smiled back weakly and then looked over at the flight engineer, who was standing at the edge of the open hatch, preparing the winch and the delivery sling it would lower. The sling looked awfully small and the winch looked a little worn, as if it was not in tip-top working order.

"I'm getting in that?" Rabb yelled, pointing at the sling.

"Oh yes, sir," the Lieutenant shouted back.

Now Harm pointed down at the huge submarine righting itself on the surface of the roiling water. "I'm getting in that to go down there?"

The copilot nodded vigorously. "That's the plan, sir." He paused a moment, then added, "Those are our orders, sir." That was just to let Harm know that they weren't really enjoying this either.

Harm shrugged and shook his head slowly. This, he thought, was one *hell* of a way to practice law.

The lowering sling was a collapsible metal seat, with four stubby petals and a spider's web of restraining straps. Although Rabb sat in it with all the joy of going to the electric chair, he could tell that it was a strong piece of equipment, durable enough to support his weight no matter the weather. It took the flight engineer a full two minutes to strap him into the thing.

As they worked every buckle and clasp, Harm studied the winch closely, as if he was looking for defects, as if he could spot some point of metal fatigue or broken gearing that had been missed by the flight crew. But he couldn't see anything wrong with it— not *really*—and he had to reassure himself with the fact that he knew that these helo crews did this kind of thing all the time. He had to believe that they knew what they were doing and that everything worked as it was supposed to.

Finally secured into the sling, Harm summoned up the courage to look down again. The Sea Stallion was doing its best to match its speed to the sub 500 feet below, and the pilot was doing his best to keep the winch hatch directly above a very small landing point on the giant submersible's conning tower. The sub pushed its way through the pounding sea, the helo stayed—as best it could—in position directly above it. Harm chanced a look down at the submarine. One glance and he got the sense that the submarine was bigger than it should have been, considering the vastness of the turbulent ocean thundering and blasting all around it.

Harm's mouth was dry with fear, but when he opened it, words managed to come tumbling out. "You're going to drop me down there? Is it safe? Haven't I seen this place somewhere before? Like in a movie? A TV show? A video game?"

The flight engineer was used to this kind of last-minute panic; he had heard it all before. "You'll be just fine, sir," he lied. "Nothing to worry about. This whole procedure has been checked out . . . very safe . . . just go with it."

Then with a push of a button and the throw of a lever, Harm was swung out of the door of the chopper and smack into the wash of the rotors and the strong rushing sea winds.

Below him—and at that moment it looked about a hundred miles below him—three people were emerging from a hatchway on the conning tower of the submarine. The garish white shaft of light from a searchlight hit him. He could see in the tunnel of light the beginning of driving rain—Harm was soaked in an instant, as if he had just strolled through a car wash. The sling was swinging like a pendulum and the roar of the helicopter engines suddenly got louder.

And that's when things got funny—at the precise moment that the flight engineer started lowering him toward the conning tower, the cell phone in Harm's breast pocket began to chirp. Just why Harm thought he had to answer it, he would never know.

Somehow he managed to reach the phone, pull it out of his pocket, and clumsily flip the device open.

It was Mac.

"My God, Harm, where are you?" Her voice sounded very small and very far away. "It sounds like you're in a subway."

The seat Harm was sitting in was spinning crazily and it was all he could do to hold the receiver to his ear. He was being buffeted by the wind and the rain was hitting him like little teeth.

"I'll explain later," he yelled. "What have you found out?"

"Only one thing, but it's kind of interesting," she replied. "Did you know that Hawkes was due to have a security review in two weeks?"

"No. So what? Everyone gets one."

"Yeah," Mac yelled back, "but the crazy thing is that he just had one. Just over a month ago."

Harm did not know that, but even in his crazy predicament, the information Mac had just relayed him gave him pause. "Really . . ." he said softly.

"What?" Mac yelled.

"He was due for *another* security review? Are you sure? You wouldn't kid me at a time like this, would you?"

"I don't know *what* you're doing, Harm," said Mac. "But I would not kid you about this."

Spinning and wet though he was, Harm's mind fastened on this surprising piece of information. All major line officers went through security review once a year, and these reviews were never pro forma affairs and could take a number of different forms. Sometimes, they were straight face-to-face interviews, with extensive, hard hitting questions. Sometimes they hooked you up to a polygraph, started with your name, and then worked their way all the way through your life and naval career. There were even dark rumors of security reviews taking place under sedation and drug-induced truth-telling. Unless you had done something stupid or seriously wrong, they—and "they" were operatives of the Naval Investigation Service—weren't looking for anything in particular. They were just nosing around, looking for weak points, indicators that things might change in the future. After every security review, your personnel file got a little fatter. Security reviews could be grueling and intrusive, but once they were done, you were clean for a year. So why then would Hawkes be called to take a review again, when he had just had one?

"Can you stay on that for me?" Harm shouted.

There was a long pause. Suddenly, Harm flashed on the overnight bag she had been carrying that morning. She had said she was going to try to get out of Washington that weekend. "Oh, sorry," he said. "You had plans. I forgot."

There was another long pause from the landward end of the connection. Harm could almost hear Mac wrestling with herself—her sense of duty struggling against her right to have a day off now and then.

Finally, she answered. "Well," Mac said, "maybe I can get someone else to follow up before I . . ." Her voice seemed to trail off—or was it the bad connection, or had it been snatched away by the roaring wind?

"Okay," Harm said quickly—he didn't want her

to finish that sentence. "Anything you can do to help, I'd appreciate, Mac."

"I'll try," she replied, and hung up.

Harm continued his precarious descent. It took another two minutes—two *long* minutes—for the sling to be lowered to the point where the men on the conning tower could snag him with a boat hook.

It took a couple of tries, but finally they hooked him like a freshly caught tuna, and pulled him into the well of the conning tower. A couple of sailors went to work on the snaps and in a matter of seconds he was free of the contraption. The chopper, very noisy now, clattered away, disappearing into the low cloud, the sling trailing away behind it like the tail of a kite. Harm, soaking wet, stared at the three men who had landed him on the submarine. They looked back at him as if expecting him to do something.

Then it hit him. "Permission to come aboard?"

The three men all saluted.

"Permission granted," one of them said. "Welcome aboard the USS *Tennessee*."

Four

THE USS TENNESSEE WAS A NUCLEAR-powered submarine armed with a variety of long-range strategic missiles, an Ohio class/Trident vessel that was part of the backbone of the U.S.'s seaborne defense. Although the missiles had no preset targets when the submarine went on patrol, the *Tennessee* was capable of rapidly targeting their missiles should the need arise, using secure and constant at-sea communications links.

The fish was enormous. Five hundred and sixty feet long, forty-two feet on the beam—the old cliché about the cramped and uncomfortable spaces on submarines did not apply. True, it wasn't a cruise ship, but there was plenty of space for the fifteen officers and 140 enlisted men who made up the company.

Although Harmon Rabb was well-traveled in the Navy, this was his first time on board a Trident-class submarine, and he was astonished by its size and complexity—he was also acutely aware that he was dripping water all over its pristine interior. Mercifully, he was relieved of his heavy weather gear by a sailor, who then lead him through the labyrinth of corridors to the Captain's Quarters.

There was almost complete silence on board as the sailors on duty went about their tasks, the only sound being the occasional beep or signal from communications equipment and the constant low hum of the submarine's two turbines.

And it was all under the command of one man, Wilcox Mattingly, who waited for Rabb in the spacious Captain's Quarters—a suite of rooms not all that much smaller than similar accommodations on the larger surface ships. He seemed amiable enough, but a stoop in his shoulders told of too many years of having his finger on the nuclear button. Added to that, one of his best friends had just died. Mysteriously.

"So," he said, with a hint of irony playing in his smile, "how was your ingress, Commander?"

Harm smiled and ran a hand through his ruffled hair. He was sure he did not present a picture of a proper Naval officer. "It's not usually the way I spend my Saturday nights, sir."

"No," said Wilcox. He poured a cup of coffee from one of the two silver thermoses on his desk, handed it to Rabb, and motioned to him to sit. "I wish we could have been in a more convenient place for you."

Harm took the coffee gratefully, gulped the scalding liquid, and felt some warmth returning to his numb body.

"I understand, sir," he said. "You were only a day out of port, so we didn't have to fly too far. And I won't take up much of your time."

Mattingly leaned back in his chair and sipped his own cup of coffee. "Well," he said. "What can I tell you?"

Harm put down his coffee and took out his notebook—it was simple force of habit—then paused, as if unsure of what to do next. Chegwidden had been quite clear on the fact that there was to be nothing on paper . . . But Harm decided to take notes anyway, just to fix the facts in his mind. He was acutely aware of Mattingly, who had obviously seen the hesitation.

"Well," said Harm briskly, as if trying to put it behind him. "Let's start with what happened the night before. Your version. In your own words."

Mattingly's face darkened slightly, as if he were about to lash out in anger, then he just shrugged. "Hell, you're just doing your job . . ."

"Yes, sir."

The Captain took a deep breath. "We got together like we do every year," he began. "We have dinner, a few drinks. We've been doing it for more than twenty-five years. This one was not much different—except McKitrick was the host this year and he put on a hell of a show. Last year—when it was my turn—I just rented a room in a restaurant in Kings Bay—that's the homeport for this vessel—and laid out a spread. This year Eric really went whole hog . . . Very lavish. On his yacht—or rather, the yacht that his agency somehow got hold of. Eric was never saltwater Navy and the rest of us had just come off ships—except for Conroy, no one *ever* knows where *he* comes from—but I guess it was Eric's way of putting on the dog. Letting us all know what a big man he is in Washington nowadays . . ."

There was just the slightest tinge of resentment in Mattingly's voice. Rather, he seemed more amused at his old friend putting on such airs and graces, considering that everybody on the yacht had known each other back when.

So far so good. Harm had read the report. McKitrick was the spook, Conroy was the SEAL.

"So apart from the location, this get-together was no different from any other, is that it?"

Mattingly nodded. "We told the same stories . . . shared the same laughs. Joe did his usual act with Hawkes, ragging the hell out of him. The only difference was, we didn't get *quite* as loaded as usual. We're getting too old for that. Next year it'll probably be lemonade and ginger ale all 'round . . ." Mattingly said with a laugh and a shake of his head.

"You'll do it next year?" Harm asked. "You'll have a dinner despite the fact that one of the original crew is missing?"

Mattingly's face fell and he seemed to wince in

pain. "Oh . . . that's right. I had forgotten about that. . . ."

"I'm sorry, sir."

Mattingly waved off the apology. "Forget it."

"What did you mean . . ." Harm glanced down at his notes. "Captain Phillips did his usual act?"

Mattingly had anticipated the question, and waved it off. "Oh, it was just the usual bull. Nothing serious."

Harm was firm. "I have to insist, sir."

Mattingly shrugged again. "It was a routine that Phillips had been doing over the last four or five years. Maybe it was beginning to get to him—but not enough to . . . Look, it was just a lot of drunken nonsense, okay, Commander."

"I have to ask you to be a bit more specific, Captain."

Mattingly put his elbows on the table. "Okay. Here we are—five guys. We all leave the academy on the same day, we have more or less the same records. We all bust ass. We all get to where we want to be—eventually—except for Phillips. He's stuck on the *Mackinac* and Hawkes and I are driving these beauties around. McKitrick is the big spook. Conroy is out doing God knows what, but he always was into that clandestine stuff. The Mac was the last stop before Joe got a carrier—and there just weren't any spaces."

"But what did he say that night?" Harm persisted. "He didn't threaten Captain Hawkes, did he?"

Mattingly fixed Harm with that look that superiors

reserve for inferior officers whom they consider pro-
foundly stupid. "No. He did not."

Harmon Rabb changed his tactic quickly. "Well,
the *Mackinac* is a pretty considerable command," he
said. "He was in line for his carrier command eventually. Surely, Captain Phillips understood that someone has to bring up the rear."

"Eventually," said Mattingly, as if tasting the
word. "Eventually is a word that can mean a hundred
years in the Navy. I'm sure as a JAG, you know that
as well as any of us."

Harm nodded. "Yes, sir I do," he said, his voice
taking on a carefully modulated tone of respect. "But
patience is also a word we all know, too isn't it?"

"Yes," said Mattingly. "And no one could accuse
Joe Phillips of not being patient. He was patient and
then some." Mattingly stared into his cooling coffee.
He looked as if he was thinking of something else,
some other incident in the long history of the five
officers.

"How do you mean?"

"Of all of us, Joe worked the hardest, I would say.
He did everything—and I mean *everything*—by the
book. He wasn't a hardass about it—he just knew the
right way and the wrong way of doing things in
the Navy and he always did the right thing. But he
had one fatal flaw. . . ."

"Sir?" Harm thought it was an odd choice of
words, considering that Phillips had not been the fa-
tality.

"He wasn't ambitious. Not until recently. He figured that if he worked hard, kept his nose clean, fol-

40

lowed the book, then the good things would follow—
a natural progression. Until the clock started ticking
on his career, Phillips never whined, never com-
plained, never pushed himself forward, never stabbed
the other guy in the back. I'm not saying you *have* to
do that to get ahead, but . . .''

Captain Mattingly left the end of the sentence hanging in the air between them: *but it sure doesn't
hurt . . .*

''You're saying everyone else cuts corners?''

Mattingly shook his head vigorously. ''No, I'm not
saying that at all. That kind of thing comes back to
bite you in the ass like a cobra.'' He leaned forward
and refilled Harm's coffee mug.

''Thank you,'' Harm said, and sipped. ''What *are*
you saying, sir?''

''What I'm saying is that Phillips may have worked
the books too hard, neglecting some other parts of the
equation. It's not *just* about being a good sailor, you
know.''

''I'm afraid I'm going to have to call for a trans-
lation on that, sir.''

''He didn't kiss ass enough,'' said Mattingly. ''Or
he didn't kiss the right ones. Is that blunt enough for
you, Commander?''

Harm nodded. Yeah, he knew all about such things.
''That's more than blunt enough for me, sir.''

''How about Captain Hawkes?'' he asked Mattingly. ''Whose behinds was he kissing?''

Mattingly continued to be blunt. ''Everyone's. Or
all the right ones. He was good at it. Much smoother
than Phillips—even though those two were the best

41

of friends. They were even neighbors for a while, when they were both posted to CINCPACFLT out in Pearl Harbor.

That unwieldy Naval acronym meant Commander in Chief, Pacific Fleet—a collection of letters that referred to a very rarefied level of the United States Navy. Phillips and Hawkes had served on the staff of the Commander in Chief of a Navy that covered the largest body of water on earth, a fighting force with personnel in the tens of thousands as well as surface ships and submersibles by the score. Even before their present commands, Hawkes and Phillips had ascended to the heights of the Naval hierarchy, stratospheric levels of the service that very few ever attained.

"Captain Phillips could retire tomorrow," said Harm slowly, "and know that he had done more than 99 percent of his fellow officers. By any measure he had made the Navy his career and had made a success of that career . . . and yet, you say he had ambition—late in life."

Mattingly rubbed his eyes vigorously, as if trying to stay awake, as if this interview had been going on for days instead of less than an hour. "I dunno, Commander. I just don't know . . . Maybe we were all to blame. We were friends at Annapolis, good friends. One for all and all for one." He smiled, his lips slightly crooked. "But maybe that was the problem. Somehow, rivalry developed . . . I envied Eric—that's Admiral McKitrick, when he made Captain. Then *I* made Captain and I'll bet Conroy was fit to bust a gut." He smiled again and almost laughed. "Joe Phillips was the first to make Commander—the first of all of us—and I'll bet you would have heard the swearing from the other four from Can Ranh Bay to Naples—or wherever the hell we were when we heard . . . Maybe we should have given up our little club a couple of years out of the Academy . . . but we didn't." Mattingly shrugged and looked tired. "Maybe the whole thing was just plain stupid. An overgrown boys' club that got to play with bigger toys. I dunno . . ." Captain Mattingly stood up. "Now a young fellow like you has to figure it all out. And I'm sorry about that. I truly am. I guess that's all."

Harm took a long pull on his lukewarm coffee, then faced his superior officer, looking him straight in the eye. "Well, actually, I'm sorry to say that I *do* have a few more questions for you, sir."

For a moment it looked as if Mattingly would pull rank, bark out a refusal, and stomp out, leaving Harm stranded in a Trident submarine in the middle of the North Atlantic, but then the older man's shoulders slumped and, looking a little defeated, he dropped back into the desk chair. His flipped his hands up, open-palmed. "Fire away, Commander."

"If we could get back to the question of Captain Hawkes and his, um, strategies for promotion."

"His ass-kissing?"

"Yes, sir. That."

Mattingly shrugged. "We've all done it. *I* have. And I know *you* have. A. J. Chegwidden is not an easy man to get around, but he does love to have his ass kissed. Am I wrong?"

Harm opened his mouth to say something but thought better of it, so he closed his mouth again.

Mattingly cackled, laughing with real amusement. "You don't think that I *don't* know your boss, do you? Hell, son, one of the first things you do when you're in a position like mine is get to know the bulldogs who are going to be sniffing at your tracks. 'Course, I've known A. J. since we were in Vietnam together. Long before he was a lawyer. Still, doesn't hurt to know the top guy in JAG—but when *I* knew him he wasn't a lawyer. He was one lethal sailor. Has he ever mentioned how many men he killed out there when he was driving Riverines?"

Harm smiled slightly. "Not in so many words, sir. But he has implied that he was . . . active. . . ."

"Well, that's all you need to know, then, I guess . . . Now what was the question, Commander?"

"Captain Hawkes," began Harmon Rabb respectfully, "and his methods for . . . preferment."

Mattingly looked disappointed, as if the tales of Admiral Chegwidden's adventures in the bloody inlets, rivers, and estuaries of North and South Vietnam was a subject more to his liking.

"Oh . . . well . . . Hawkes went to all the right parties. He had—has—a beautiful wife, Angie her name is, and she comes from money. Southern money. She knew how to charm the right Admiral's wife, have the perfect luncheon. And Hawkes was right there, kissing the right ass, greasing the right wheel . . . Now don't get me wrong, Al Hawkes was a great sailor, a *great* sailor. I'd trust him with my life. He knew everything that had to be known to run a tight ship. And he could fly, too. So, a combination of skill, expertise, ass-kissing, and Angie—they were an unbeatable couple, an unbeatable combination . . . together they were just plain *better* at the PR game than Joe and Sylvia. And, in the end, that's how Al Hawkes got his carrier first. It's the kind of thing that happens every day in the Navy, son. I'll bet your wife knows that.'' Mattingly leaned forward and looked conspiratorial. ''In fact, I'd bet it was your wife that helped you up to your rank. Am I wrong?''

In fact, Captain Mattingly was wrong. ''Well, the truth of it is . . . I'm not married, Captain.''

''Well,'' said Mattingly in deadly earnest. ''If you *were* married and to the *right* girl, you would have made Captain by now.''

''Well . . .'' said Harm, ''I don't know about that, sir . . .'' Suddenly he had the feeling he was humoring the man. It was time for a change of tactic. ''Tell me about Colonel Conroy and Admiral McKitrick. How did they get along with Captain Hawkes? Or Captain Phillips, for that matter?''

''Great,'' said Mattingly stoutly. ''Absolutely great. I don't suppose you went to the Academy, Rabb, but I don't think you understand the bond that exists between classmates, friends, comrades-in-arms . . .''

Rabb was wearing a U.S. Naval Academy ring the size of a horseshoe on his ring finger, and was surprised that Mattingly had not noticed it. ''Well,'' he said. ''In actual fact, I'm—''

''I mean,'' interrupted Mattingly, ''being a SEAL

and a Marine, Conroy can be intense. McKitrick is, well . . . He's a spook. He knows where all the bodies are buried . . . And now there's one more. My old pal Al Hawkes . . .''

For one terrible moment, it looked to Harm as if Captain Mattingly was going to cry. But Mattingly contained himself.

"When are the services?" Mattingly asked after a moment or two.

"They are keeping Captain Hawkes's death under wraps for the time being," Harm replied. "After that, I'm sure that the body will be released and that arrangements will be made for a proper burial."

Mattingly did not look at Harm; he seemed to be staring at a knot in the wood of his desktop. "It's strange . . ." he began.

"What's strange, sir?"

"We were such good friends . . . We've known each other since we were kids, beginners." Mattingly pulled his head back and stared at the ceiling. Rabb saw the tears in his eyes and he could have sworn that the Captain had been drinking. But alcohol was forbidden on capital ships of the U.S. Navy, except on special occasions—and this interview, most decidedly, was not one of them.

Then Harm realized why there were two carafes of coffee. His cup had always been poured from one, Mattingly's from the other.

"We've known each other for so long and I don't think any of us will be able to make the funeral." Mattingly took a long swig of his cold coffee. "Well," he added, "Maybe McKitrick."

Harm looked across the expanse of desk. "That may be true, sir. But you will have to make it to the investigative hearing."

Mattingly sat bolt upright, as if he had been doused with cold seawater. If he was drunk, he was hiding it well. He blinked twice. "Well, I guess that's completely correct, Commander Rabb," he said with exaggerated preciseness, as if spelling out each word before he spoke it. "When is it? And where will it be?"

Harm shook his head. "That is up to NIS," he said evenly. "But I would guess that it will be sooner rather than later. Once the press—and the rest of the world—gets hold of this, well, sir, I think the Navy will want it wrapped up pretty damn quick. If not, the fallout—"

"Yeah, I know," said Mattingly. "Then it will be coming down in buckets. Right?"

"Something like that, sir."

Mattingly smiled and slopped some more coffee into his cup. He did not offer Harm any. "Right. Something like that." He sipped the coffee, then squared his shoulders. "Now—is there anything else I can do for you, Commander Rabb? Any blank spots that need to be filled in?"

Harm didn't have to think. "Just one last thing, sir," he said evenly. "Do you think Captain Phillips killed Captain Hawkes?"

Mattingly answered instantly. "No. I don't. But that's just my opinion, Commander. I'll let *you* find out the honest-to-goodness truth."

• • • •

The process of getting *from* a submarine *into* a Sea Stallion was just as unpleasant, cold, and hair-raising as the opposite maneuver, with the possible exception that this time Harm had a vague notion of what was going to happen to him. Furthermore, he was not distracted by sudden cell phone communication from Sarah. Once he was back in the safety—such as it was—of the Sea Stallion battling headwinds and a weather depression as it made its way back to Andrews, he thought about what he had been told on the submarine. Five friends, five ambitious men, five men striving for the brassiest ring the Navy could hand them. Those five men had worked hard—fought, killed, for the U.S. Navy—and they did it for honor, for country . . . and advancement, too. They wanted to succeed and each one of them had very specific goals. Four had made it, one had not . . . Had one died for the other's failure?

Harmon Rabb had been an outstanding graduate of the United States Naval Academy, Annapolis, Maryland. He had been ranked high in his class, but one of many very qualified, highly motivated graduates. Of the 230 midshipmen of his year, he didn't know one who hadn't bragged that he was going to command *this* carrier or *that* sub . . . this one was going to be CNO, another was going to go all the way to the Joint Chiefs. Harmon Rabb had been ambitious, too. He was going to fly carrier-based Navy jets—just as his father had done—but when his night vision problem washed him out of that option, he set himself to be the best lawyer JAG could offer.

He couldn't quite understand the rivalry of the four

officers he was supposed to question. Maybe there were other members of his class keeping score, but he wasn't. Not anymore. Not since he had been grounded.

Five ✈

HARMON RABB MADE IT BACK TO JAG
headquarters early Sunday morning. After his two
chopper rides and the ascents and descents in between, he felt as if he had been in a fight then put to
bed in a blender, but he was in one piece and still
breathing. A small victory.

There was a surprise waiting for him in his office.
Mac. She was still there. She was dressed differ-
ently—her overnight bag was open on the floor next
to her desk, and Harm guessed that she was working

51

her way through her weekend wardrobe without going home.

"What are you doing here?" he asked, genuinely astonished to see her.

"I've been going through your cable traffic ever since you left," she said without looking up from the mess of papers spread out before her. She sounded more than a little annoyed. "They've been flooding in since you walked out the door. All of them security level seven. I had to get clearance from Chegwidden before I could open them."

Harm frowned. That piece of information told him that the Admiral had probably not left the building in twenty-four hours, either. That would make for a very unhappy Admiral.

The thick dossiers of the five officers still sat on his desk, and for a moment he wished he had stayed and read them instead of haring off to the *Tennessee*. "I wonder if there's anything here that would tell us why Hawkes had that second security review."

Now Mac looked up and grimaced. "From the size of those things there's probably a report on his first diaper change," she said. "It's got to be in there somewhere."

Then the phone rang—it was as if someone was following Harm's movements and knew the instant he had arrived back in Falls Church. Mac answered it—just as she had done before—and had the same look on her face when she handed Harm a note.

"Well it looks like your exciting weekend isn't over yet," she said. Then she looked ruefully at her overnight bag. "Though I have a feeling that mine is."

"Now what?" Harm asked. He really did feel bad about Sarah's lost weekend, but a Captain of a carrier didn't get killed every day of the week. Thank God, he added silently.

"There will be a car downstairs in two minutes," she said. "You're supposed to get in it . . . I have a feeling you are about to go meet an Admiral."

"McKitrick?"

Mac nodded. "The same."

Harmon Rabb's shoulders slumped. "But who'll go through all this paper? The key could be in there."

"Who'll go through it?" said Mac. "Who do you think?"

Harm could have kissed her—but he didn't. "I'll be back as soon as I can, okay? Thanks, Mac."

No one had told him anything about it, but he knew the car that was waiting for him the moment he saw it. In a lot full of government-issue Chryslers, Fords, and Chevrolets, the huge, black Cadillac limousine stood out like an ocean liner in the middle of a fishing fleet.

The driver was in uniform, a servant's livery—dark suit, white shirt, tie, peaked cap—but there was something military about him. Harmon sensed that he was Navy, but there was no insignia to prove it. He knew who Harm was, too, wordlessly opening the rear door. Harm slipped into the back—the interior seemed like the size of a studio apartment—the chauffeur got up front, and off they went.

The rear of the limo was filled with the playthings that the rich and important think they need in the back of a car. A bank of phones, a fax machine, a computer, not one but three television sets, as well as the usual niceties like a bar and a refrigerator. But oddly enough, despite all this luxury, Harm could feel the weight of the car—it rode like a tank. This wasn't the kind of limo that Johnny rented to impress his date on prom night; this thing was armored. The car was bullet- and bomb-proof, right down to the tires, which were probably steel-covered with rubber so they couldn't be shot out. This was the kind of car the President would ride in— or a very important Admiral. Despite all the security, there was something about a car like this that made Harm feel like he was being set up as a target, a sitting duck.

The chauffeur's voice came through a loudspeaker somewhere in the padded walls of the compartment.

"Is everything all right, Commander? Would you like some more air-conditioning back there?"

"No. I'm fine," Harm replied. "If I asked you where you were taking me, would you tell me?"

"No, sir. I wouldn't."

"I didn't think so." Harm lay back on the soft seats and tried to relax. On the whole, though, he was more at ease getting on to the USS *Tennessee*.

There were many spook castles around Washington D.C. Langley, of course. The NSA complex. The vast new building at NRO. DIA—the so-called "puzzle palace." USAFI. The alphabet soup of buildings that officially didn't exist went all the way from A to Z and back again. Unofficial though they may have been, the places were well-known and could be found on most road maps. Hell, the CIA at Langley even offered tours. But there were other, even *more* unofficial buildings scattered here and there in Virginia, intelligence installations that were not public knowledge, did not show up on road maps, and most definitely did not offer tours.

One of them, just outside the picturesque town of Front Royal, Virginia, right at the head of the Shenandoah Valley—a long way from official Washington—was a complex of buildings known as Research Section Number Six, but the spook world knew it as Navy Combat Intelligence Systems, the inner sanctum of Naval Intelligence, the most secret place operated by the service. What was inside those buildings was known only to a few select people—the President was, grudgingly, one of them, but the Vice President was not. Despite the name, no scientific research went on here—rather, it was about game-playing and role-playing, the constant refinement of the actions of the men and women who made war at sea.

It was with some surprise to Harm to discover that Research Section Number Six *actually* was a castle, or a reasonable nineteenth-century facsimile of one, one of the great lodges or country houses built by robber barons at the end of last century. The gates were massive, wrought-iron confections—ornate, baroque barriers of black iron and gold gilt, topped by two globe lights and manned by two no-nonsense Navy shore patrolmen. They knew the driver and he knew them, but that didn't stop them from going through a battery of security procedures necessary to gate entrance. There was a check of ID cards, of course, as well as a thumbprint identification, followed by a series of code words. Apparently Harm and the driver passed, and the great gates swung open.

Research Center Number Six sat atop a hill in the middle of several hundred acres of field, forest, and, nearer the building itself, well-tended gardens and lawns. Harm nodded to himself—it fit right in with the picture of McKitrick Harm had half-assembled in his mind. The yacht, the castle—McKitrick liked his comforts and he did not care who paid for them. The building itself was made of heavy granite and was as crenellated and turreted as any medieval castle, the lower parts of the walls covered with a thick growth of ivy. The only thing that suggested the twentieth century was the thick array of aerials and satellite dishes that were spread across the Castle's spires and slates.

Two more plainclothes guards were waiting at the thick, black oak door which swung open automatically as the driver and Harm approached. The driver and the two guards gestured him in, and Harm stepped from the nineteenth century into something approaching the twenty-first.

Despite the medieval aspect outside, the inside resembled the interior of the combat control center from some vast, land-bound ship. There were banks of computer screens and printers quietly spitting out information. There were people in uniform, working at keyboards and frowning at VDT screens. Things were quiet and controlled, as if everyone knew exactly what task to perform and when. No one paid any attention to Harm and his escort.

An attractive female ensign appeared and smiled a perfect, dazzling smile. "Commander Rabb? This way, please."

They climbed a wooden staircase of baronial dimension—the walls decorated with vast, dark seascapes, no doubt on loan from the National Gallery of Art—to a second floor, where they made another century-shift. They were back in the old-fashioned world of the original house. Between large rectangular islands of thick Persian carpets, the parquet floors were polished to a high gloss. They walked directly down the wide corridor to the last door. It was unmarked. The ensign opened it, smiled that fabulous smile again, and then disappeared.

A secretary sat at a desk, working at a computer. She was not the dazzling creature that the ensign had been, but an older, sort of tough-looking civilian woman. A filled ashtray on her cluttered desk told Harm all he needed to know about her. If she was prepared to disobey the fiercely imposed ban on smoking in government buildings, then there was no doubt in his mind that she was one hard lady. And she was probably McKitrick's watchdog and tough-cookie mother-figure.

"Rabb?" she said, squinting through a pall of smoke from an Old Gold.

"That's right, ma'am."

She cocked her head toward the double doors behind her. "He's in there. Don't bother knocking."

The office was huge, a giant rectangular room with one wall given over to windows with spectacular views down the Shenandoah Valley, another holding bookshelves large enough to stock a small-town library. A wood and brass ladder on well-worn tracks allowed access to the higher volumes, and a spiral staircase led to an upper gallery.

McKitrick sat at the far end of the room behind a desk that would only have fit in a room that size. McKitrick was small and wiry, well-tanned, a man who spent a lot of time in the sun, unlike Mattingly. He was wearing half-frame glasses on the end of his nose, and they gave him the air of a slightly dotty college professor. But the glittering, sharp eyes behind the lenses dispelled that notion immediately. They were eyes, Harm could tell, that did not miss much.

The Admiral accepted Harm's salute, then half-rose in his padded desk chair, reaching across the expanse of mahogany to shake hands. In that moment of contact, McKitrick looked Harm over quickly, as if reading him, something that spooks always did, as if after a single glance, they knew you better than you did yourself. Of course, Harm had no doubt that the Admiral *did* know a great deal about Lieutenant Commander Harmon Rabb. He had probably been reading his file all morning long.

"Nice ride out?" McKitrick asked. He almost—but not quite—managed to sound as if he cared.

"Very nice, sir."

McKitrick sat back in his chair. "What do you

think of our little setup out here? Cozy, isn't it?''

"Very nice," said Harm again. "It looks like it might beat working inside the Beltway."

McKitrick smiled. "Oh, you'd be surprised. I miss the excitement of downtown D.C. from time to time. Besides, the food out here is awful."

Harm was sure that McKitrick wasn't roughing it all that much. Someplace, no doubt, in this castle, was a kitchen and in that kitchen was bound to be a chef, not some ham-fisted cook from the Quartermaster Corps. Besides, if the food on site got boring, Harm happened to know that the Virginia hills were home to a number of very expensive and rather exclusive inns—all of which had four-star restaurants attached.

Harm, of course, was not going to contradict a Flag-ranked officer to his face. "Well, I guess you can't send out for pizza, this establishment being secret."

"Yes," McKitrick agreed. "It's a pretty exciting place to be. Even if it is buried in the middle of nowhere."

Of course, Harm was dying to ask just what the hell everyone was doing in this place, but he knew that even if he had the nerve to ask, McKitrick would not tell him a thing.

Instead, he said, "Well, sir, you know why I'm here."

"Yes," replied McKitrick, taking the glasses from his nose and rubbing his eyes vigorously. "I haven't been able to sleep since I heard about it. Such a shock. And such a waste."

"Hawkes *and* Phillips?" said Harm, surprised at

59

the Admiral's rush to judgment. "You seem pretty sure that Captain Phillips is guilty. Why is that?"

McKitrick just smiled, leaned back in his chair, and busied himself filling a pipe from an old pouch. He made a great show of lighting it, sending clouds of smoke spiraling toward the ornate ceiling. It seemed that Federal Government rules ended well before they got to the Admiral's desk.

"Do you have any idea what we do here, Commander Rabb?"

Rabb could take a big fat guess, but decided to go limp. "That would be classified well above my clearance, sir."

"That's a very diplomatic answer, Commander." McKitrick smiled around the stem of his pipe. "You probably think it has something to do with surveillance and wiretap . . . Monitoring the movement of foreign vessels, tracking men and women we think might be working against our interests . . . that sort of thing."

Harm shrugged. "Well . . ."

McKitrick waved the pipe at him, erasing his thoughts in a puff of smoke. "We study one thing here, Commander Rabb. Logic. Not rumor. Not human intelligence or satellite photos. We deal in logic, the way one plays a chess game, anticipating actions a hundred, two hundred moves in advance. In a matter such as this, the logic points to a series of events, wouldn't you say?"

"Perhaps you could fill me in, sir."

McKitrick thrust a thumb into his pipe, found that it was still lit and puffed away for a moment. "Two men," he said. "Rivals in their careers. Rivals in their personal life. Add alcohol. Add opportunity." McKitrick shrugged. "You have to admit that there is a logical conclusion that can be drawn from those simple facts."

Harm's sense of diplomacy slipped slightly. "These men were supposed to be friends of yours," Harm said. It looked like the Admiral had Hawkes buried and Phillips convicted. So much for those sleepless nights . . .

"They were," the Admiral said through a cloud of thick cherry blend. That's why I haven't been sleeping. Being logical about this does not mean that one is without feelings. If I have to tell the President something . . . unpleasant . . . like that a preemptive strike of a hostile nation will costs the lives of 20,000 noncombatants, I feel for those people. You may not believe that, Commander, but that does not concern me."

"You said Hawkes and Phillips were personal as well as professional rivals. What did you mean by that? I thought they were friends—I thought you were all friends."

"We, they were . . . we are," McKitrick said. "Mostly. There have been ups and downs over the years. Stands to reason that there would be. I'm sure that you've had similar problems with old friends . . . I imagine no one has told you about the wives."

"Wives?"

McKitrick grinned, a little cruelly, Harm thought. Harm noticed that the Admiral was not wearing a wedding band.

"Many years ago . . . I don't think any one of us had made Captain. One night the San Diego police found Phillips and Hawkes fighting on Hawkes's front lawn. Can you imagine what that was about?"

Harm only had to consider the question for a second or two. "Who caught whom?"

McKitrick smiled again. "Well, that's classified. But off the record, we heard that they caught each other."

It took Harm a few more seconds to decipher this. McKitrick's eyebrows arched, as if he was surprised that it was taking Harm so long to figure out the simple equation.

"They were cheating with each others wives?" he said.

"Well, like I say . . . that's classified." McKitrick seemed to be enjoying this rather more than he should have.

"One question for you, sir?"

"Yes?"

"Where were you on the night of the murder?"

"I beg your pardon?"

"After the dinner? Where did you go? Did you go into Newport News with the others?"

"Oh no. I stayed on the boat and we turned around and sailed home."

"We?"

"It carries a crew of seven, plus the stewards. I even took the bridge for an hour or two . . . I'm sure it's in the logs of the Cats Paw II, which is, you should know, a serving ship in the United States

Navy.'' McKitrick sat back and puffed on his pipe. It was his nice, logical way of saying he was not guilty of the death of Alan Hawkes. He couldn't be. He had a watertight alibi.

six

HARM HARDLY NOTED THE RIDE BACK TO
Falls Church; he was thinking too hard. During his
time in the service of his country, he had been forced
to learn to use his instincts, but not to go overboard
on hunches. If Freud's cigar really was sometimes just
a cigar, so spies spied, men cheated, sometimes they
got murdered by someone who wanted their wallet.

McKitrick knew much and he didn't mind letting
you know he knew. McKitrick knew much, but had
actually said very little. Was the information he had
really off-limits to Harm and his investigation, or was
he simply concealing his own connection to the murder? There again . . . there was that alibi.

As the limousine reached the Beltway, Harm
looked out the tinted window to see that a large, black

thundercloud had positioned itself over the city. A moment later there were flashes of lightning, and he could hear the rumble of thunder, even through the bulletptoof glass.

A thunderstorm. In October? Now *that* defied logic. But it was happening nonetheless.

There were only a few people hanging around JAG headquarters, the rain was pouring down, and the air was muggy and oppressive—more like a Washington July than Fall. Harm got soaked in the short sprint from the limousine to the door of the office building, and he felt the weight of the investigation on his shoulders, hanging as wet and spongy as his sodden clothes. In his own office, he found a small sliver of light and welcome, one that lifted his spirits to no end.

Mac was still there. She was behind his desk, her hair a little mussed, her sweater off. She had a mountain of notes in front of her. She shifted the phone to the other ear as he came in, barely looking up at him. She pointed vigorously at the coffee machine on top of the filing cabinet. She was not suggesting that Harm get himself a cup. Rather, she was telling him to make a new batch of coffee. Still in his McKitrick mode, Harm told himself that this was a logical conclusion: she has drunk an entire pot of coffee in the course of doing his work for him.

He started a particularly strong pot. By the time he was finished, she was off the phone.

"Did you go for a limo ride?" Mac asked.

"I cannot tell a lie," said Harm.

"To Spy Heaven?"

Harm poured himself a cup of coffee and felt a hot caffeine jolt almost immediately. "Well, I have to admit that that is the perfect name for it," he said. "But it only made the picture more cloudy. Even though I got a lesson in drawing logical conclusions."

"Cloudy? Really?" She sipped from the cup he had handed her, and hardly winced. "Well, read this—guaranteed you won't like the forecast."

Harm took the fax she held in her hand. It was the preliminary autopsy report on Hawkes. A simple bullet to the heart. Small caliber cheap handgun. The bullet had entered just below the third rib and had done some serious internal damage before ending up in his heart, blowing it to pieces.

"A pretty shoddy piece of shooting," Harm said, noting that the personal effects had included a wallet but no money or credit cards. "Could it be that Allan Hawkes, Grand Old Sea Warrior, was returning home, was confronted by some second-rate criminal who pulled a gun on him, but the Grand Old Sea Warrior had a bellyful of booze, which, as you know, makes you impervious to bullets . . . Could he have just been mugged?"

"Or could it have been a trained killer?" Mac asked.

"Come on," said Harm skeptically. "Why would you say that?"

"Well," she said, handing him a piece of paper, "You can ask that question yourself."

It was another piece of yellow cable paper. "I think you're going on another trip," she said.

"Not so soon," he protested, taking the paper from

her. He scanned it. It was from Chegwidden. The page was filled with unscrambled security codes and transfer edits, but it was clear that the Old Man had opened another door for Harm. But once again, Harm could only see murkiness on the other side.

"Where the hell do they want me to go now?"

"Last paragraph," Mac said. "Last sentence."

Harm read it and then slumped into a chair. "They have got to be kidding me this time."

She smiled at him again and sipped her coffee. "That would *not* be the logical conclusion," she said.

The weather was still stormy when he took off from Andrews later that evening. It was even stormier when they entered Cuban airspace. The weather system that had brought such misery to Washington was a storm that had begun in the south Atlantic and worked its way through the Caribbean. In contrast to Washington, this was typical late hurricane season weather and the Cubans knew how to deal with the wind and rain that had been bombarding the island all day long.

As a precaution, the small Cuban Navy had put to sea early in the morning, running ahead of the storm and into the calmer waters of the mid-Atlantic. The Air Force had been wheeled back into the hangars— not that there was much flying being done by the last Communist Air Force on earth. There was such a shortage of spare parts and fuel that the Cubans had trouble keeping more than five or six planes in the air at any one time.

Citizens of the island had been told to expect a

power blackout at eight that evening and, promptly, every light in Havana and across the island blinked out at that time. Candles and generators were the only sources of light on the island.

Most of it, anyway. At the far eastern end of the long narrow island there was one patch of light in the swirl of the storm—this was the United States of America's foothold in one of the last shreds of the Communist world: the Guantanamo Bay Naval Base. Almost in defiance, this tiny foothold of the U.S. Navy was lit up bright, like a neon sign advertising capitalism.

The base site was tiny, an isolated installation in the lower southeast corner of an island in Guantanamo Bay and had been a tiny piece of the United States Navy since it was acquired in 1903 as a coaling station. For a long time, "GTMO" was known as the best-kept secret in the Navy, pleasant, less-than-onerous duties to be carried out in a pleasant tropical climate. Those posted to this pleasant spot, for some reason, qualified for "hardship pay."

They started earning that pay after the Cuban revolution, when Fidel Castro found the notion of the U.S. Navy occupying a piece of his country extremely galling. Harassments, both petty and major, had been meted out to GTMO ever since, but the U.S. had no intention of giving up the base (it is leased in perpetuity) because it was essential to Naval operations in the Caribbean, and because it seemed to annoy Castro so much.

The waters of the bay flow between two sides of the base—the leeward side housing the airfield, the windward used for ships. Hitting the leeward side in the dark in a storm would require a pretty good pilot. Harmon Rabb, strapped into the belly of a C-130 Hercules cargo plane, stared out the fist-sized window, but could barely make out the twin strings of runway lights. He hoped the guy up front driving knew what he was doing.

He tried to reassure himself. *Only a "Herk" would fly in weather as awful as this,* he thought as he tightened his already taut security harness. The Herk was as strong as a Mack truck, if somewhat easier to fly. Still, he couldn't worry about it too much—he was dog-tired.

Rabb had managed to have enough time for a shower, a shave, and a change of clothes, but he could feel the fatigue deep in his bones. Where he had been in the last forty-eight hours, the people he had spoken to—all of it whirled together in his mind and he had to shake his head periodically to keep it all straight.

The plane had been waiting for him at 1400 hours; the crew had hustled him aboard, strapped him in, and handed him a couple of ancient dog-eared copies of *Sports Illustrated* to keep him busy. He had then been bumped, bronked, and jostled all over the sky for the next six hours. He appeared to be the only passenger and/or piece of cargo.

Through his fatigue—probably because of it—he was getting angry, annoyed as hell with his assignment, furious at Hawkes for getting himself murdered, and at the murderer for having done it in the first place.

And what awaited him down there—he didn't even want to think about that.

The C-130 was a hell of an airplane. That's what Harm kept telling himself as the beast fell out of the sky, barreling through the bad weather. The four prop engines were absolutely screaming, the wings wagging this way and that. Harm sat as still as he could, as if he would upset some delicate balance that was keeping the Herk in the air and under control if he moved too much. He heard the engines retreat a little and then felt the bump and bounce as the wheels touched the tarmac of the landing strip.

The Herk pilots hit the brakes hard, and suddenly Harm felt like he was in a tractor trailer as the huge airplane careened down the runway. But the Herk was a good airplane and the pilots who flew it were top-notch—weren't they? The swinging and swaying stopped fairly quickly, and soon all Harm was aware of was the roaring wind and the rain thundering down on the skin of the C-130.

The flight engineer made his way aft and handed him a disposable plastic poncho. Harm took the thin sheet in his hands and looked dubiously at the FE.

"It's not much, Commander. But I guess it's better than nothing."

As he spoke, the side access door of the C-130 opened up and Harm found himself staring down at two of the largest human beings he had ever seen— with regard to both height and width. Both were dressed in unmarked camos, their faces blackened. Both were soaked to the skin, but did not appear to

71

have noticed. They might as well have used their face black to write "SEALs" across their foreheads.

"Commander Rabb?" one asked, as both men ripped off perfect salutes.

Harm managed a nod.

"Can you come with us, sir?"

Oh, thought Harm, groaning inwardly. This is going to be good . . .

If anything, the rain was coming down harder as the Hum Vee bearing Harm and the two SEALs splashed its way through the night.

They had left G-Base thirty minutes before and had been slithering along a serpentine mud track ever since. The road was narrow and visibility was just about zero, but the pair of rock-jawed SEALs seemed unperturbed about it, and showed no more emotion than if they were out for a Sunday drive. One drove, the other navigated, and even though Harm had heard both of them speak, he noticed that they seemed to prefer to communicate with gestures and grunts— which was fine with Harm. He was in no mood for conversation. If you're tired enough, even the hard seats of a Hum Vee can be slept on. Harm dozed off, but not before thinking that he was surprised that the U.S. territory in Guantanamo Bay was so extensive.

Then he was wide awake. GTMO was tiny—he had never been there before, but knew it was not much bigger than the deck of a carrier. They weren't in Guantanamo—they were in *Cuba*.

The Hummer came to an abrupt halt. Harm looked

around. All he could see was dark, dripping vegetation.

"Now what?" he asked.

"We have to hoof it from here, sir."

Harm did not want to get out of the Hum Vee, he did not want to climb into the wet PVC poncho—but he was damned if he would be shown up by a pair of SEALs. Of course, both men could kill him with a credit card or a spoon, carry more weight on their backs than a pair of pack mules, but he was damned if he was going to let them show him up with a little walk in the dark, the *very wet* dark.

He followed the two men through some thick undergrowth, the warm smell of tropical vegetation filling his nostrils. His feet sunk in the soft ground. The water in the stream they forded was surprisingly cold and actually felt a little refreshing in the humid air. Off in the distance he could hear a distinct booming sound. Thunder, he wondered, or artillery? Was this some hush-hush action, a mixing-it-up between the U.S. and Cuba, something that both sides agreed would never make the papers? Harm did not know. He was not sure he wanted to.

After fifteen minutes of wet, sloppy hoofing, the three men reached a clearing and the two SEALs disappeared. It was weird. One moment they were there, then in an instant they were gone.

A second later, Harm felt a yank on his pants leg. He looked down, and saw no fewer than six blackened faces looking up at him.

"Excuse me, sir," said one of them quietly. "But you are standing on my hand."

• • •

Five minutes later, Harm was sipping a cup of coffee. He was inside a hooch—an underground combination gun position, hiding place, and recon post that the SEALs were famous for building just about anywhere.

The little subterranean room was big enough to hold about a dozen men, all their equipment, their weapons, a food-storage locker, a field computer, and a mini satellite dish that could contact any point on the face of the earth. And there was a coffee pot, filled with good coffee. All of this had been put together in a matter of minutes—and yet unless you were really looking for it, this hideaway could not be found.

Sitting cross-legged on the floor was Steven Conroy—Marine Colonel, celebrated SEAL, and one of the members of the Davey Jones Locker Club.

"Of course, I was shocked when I heard about Hawkes," he said. "I've known him for most of my life—since we were scrubs at the Academy. Hell, we cleaned heads with toothbrushes together. We ran Riverine boats in 'Nam. I was there when his first kid was born and *he's* the unofficial godfather to my kid." Conroy stroked his chin and shook his head slowly, as if he still could not believe that Allan Hawkes was dead. Murdered, yet. He was silent a long time.

"It was like losing a brother, a close friend, and a colleague all at the same time," he said finally.

Harm was only half paying attention to him. He was intrigued by the hooch, intrigued by his location. He knew it would be considerably uncool to ask what the SEALs were doing here, in what had to be a significant distance inside Cuban territory; but he was itching to ask.

However, the investigation came first. "Did you detect anything unusual that night when you were all together?"

"Unusual?" Conroy repeated. "No. Nothing unusual. The drinks were packed. The food was great. The stories were the same. Same old thing, I would say."

"No arguments?" The questions were coming by rote now, but they had to be asked.

"Only whether or not the Redskins would make it to the play-offs—in fact, that wasn't even an argument. The general consensus was no, they wouldn't." Conroy's smile seemed very bright in the middle of his blacked-out face.

Harm wondered why he had not mentioned Phillips and his insistence on getting a carrier. "No arguments?"

"Nope."

"You don't recall Captain Phillips complaining that Hawkes had received command of the *Eisenhower* and he was stuck on the *Mackinac*?" Harm asked, bearing down a little.

"Oh hell, son," said Conroy with a low laugh. "That's not an argument. That's just the same old bull Joe trots out every year. Like a party trick or an old joke or something like that."

"Who *do* you think murdered Captain Hawkes, Colonel?" Harm asked slowly. It was hard to look him in the eye. His eyes were lost in the black face.

75

The SEAL officer just shrugged. "I know what I want you to tell me, Commander." Conroy wasn't laughing or even smiling anymore.

"What would that be, sir?"

"I want you to tell me it was a civilian. A mugger. Or a crackhead," he growled. Harm knew instinctively that he would *not* want to be on the other side of a reaming from this man.

Before Harm could answer, three SEALs dropped into the hooch. He had not heard them coming, hadn't even known they were there until they were . . . well, *there*. These three seemed even bigger and darker than the others. More wet, too.

One made his way directly to Conroy. "Sir, we have a—" he shot a sidelong glance at Harm. Probably never before in the history of the SEALs had a JAG officer been in a hooch, during a night operation in hostile territory. Harm could not help but feel like an interloper, a desk jockey from Washington, the kind of sailor that men like these cursed and made jokes about.

"We have a situation, sir," the SEAL finished. "You might want to come forward to take a look, sir."

Conroy shrugged and strapped on his helmet. More gunfire or thunder was booming dully in the far distance. All of the SEALs in the hooch were grabbing equipment and weapons. Noiselessly, they slithered out of the hooch.

"Two of you stay," said Conroy. Instantly, two men froze. "I want you to take the Commander here back to GTMO. See that he gets on the plane safe and sound. Understood?''

''Yes, sir,'' the two men said as if they were sharing the same brain. Both looked disappointed at being left out of the mysterious situation that was happening somewhere even deeper in Cuba.

At the entrance of the hooch, Conroy stopped, turned, and shook Rabb's hand. ''Is there going to be a formal investigation?''

Harm thought the question pretty naive. ''There will be, yes. I have no idea when or where, sir.''

''But you'll be there, right?''

''Yes, sir.''

''Well, I guess I'll be seeing you, then.'' With that, Conroy slithered out of the hooch and vanished into the dark, rainswept night.

seven

MAC RAN UP THE STAIRS TO THE TOP FLOOR

of JAG headquarters. It was 6:00 A.M. Monday morning and apart from a few quick naps on the office couch and a few brief breaks for meals, Sarah MacKenzie had been hard at it all weekend. She glanced at her watch, acutely aware that at any moment the first wave of sailors would be showing up for work on a bright, sunny Monday morning, all dressed in neatly pressed uniforms, perfect specimens of military office workers. And she looked a wreck.

She was amazed when she had gotten the call from Admiral Chegwidden. Either he had been in all night as she had, or he had snuck in while she had been dozing around dawn. She smeared on a touch of lipstick, ran her fingers through her hair, and raced for the stairs.

Mac breezed through Chegwidden's outer office door, fully expecting to see an empty waiting room. She could not have been more wrong. The place was full—every seat. Most of the people in the room were military. The couple of civilians each seemed to be clutching a briefcase or sheaf of papers. She stood openmouthed in the middle of the room as a couple of men jumped to their feet to offer her a seat. But as soon as the secretary saw her, she buzzed her straight into Chegwidden's inner sanctum.

The moment Mac saw the Admiral, she knew. He had been there all night, maybe, like her, all weekend. Chegwidden looked devastated by worry and fatigue. He looked old. He didn't stand up, he didn't salute. All he did was look at her for a moment and say "Mac, I have a favor to ask you."

Any discomfort she felt at being in the Admiral's presence out of uniform—in jeans and a tee shirt, yet—were washed away by the sound of his voice. She had never seen her superior officer look anything like this.

"Yes, sir," she answered as smartly as she could. "Anything, sir."

Chegwidden let out a long sigh, part relief, part exhaustion. "I want you to watch over an old friend of mine," the Admiral said. "An old friend who is in a bit of trouble, just at the moment."

"Sir? Who is it?"

The Admiral indicated with his chin, pointing to a far corner of the room. It was only then that Mac realized there was a third person in the office with them. If a person could be at attention and be sitting down at the same time, he was doing it. He was in dress blues, his hat resting on his knees. He, too, looked extremely worried.

The Admiral began introductions, but they were not needed. Mac knew who it was. It was Captain Joseph Phillips—suspect number one.

The USS *Mackinac* was nearly as long as an aircraft carrier, so large, in fact, that it took up not one but three of the largest berths in the Newport News docking facility. It was not a graceful-looking craft in the least; rather, the *Mac* looked like a road construction project mounted on a vast gray hull. From bow to stern it seemed to be a forest of cranes, winches, booms, and king posts. It was being loaded at the moment—loading never stopped when the ship was in port, and the extra day or two of the investigation had allowed that much more time to pack that much more cargo into the ship. The USS *Mackinac* never sailed unless it was as low in the water as it could go. There was enough cargo still stacked on the dock to provision a small town. Mac had been around more than a few Navy vessels—supercarriers included—but she had never had the feeling of being on a ship so big, so immense . . . so ugly. It would come as no surprise to Mac to learn that the ship was known to the crew as the Big Mac or TUSN—pronounced Too-sin—which stood for The Ugliest Ship in the Navy.

The USS *Mackinac* was one-of-a-kind, or, more

precisely, the last of a kind. The big cargo vessel was the last of the Sacramento-class ships designed to carry oil, ammunition, and basic cargo all in one. They were built for speed, too, giving them the ability to reprovision a fast-moving carrier without having to slow down the fight ship as it sped to a mission. As a result, the top speed of the Big Mac— as with other supercarriers—was a deeply guarded secret.

But Big Mac sailors could tell tales of seeing the immense, ghostly image of a supercarrier passing them in the night. The engineers down in the Mac engine room knew that they could have pushed their own vessel a few more clicks up and caught the haughty fighting ship in a rundown.

A JAG staff car dropped them at the base of the main ramp of the ship, and Sarah could feel Phillips tense slightly, then breathe deeply before opening the door. The decks and the dock swarmed with naval personnel—mostly plain old swabbies in fatigues working under the command of CPOs and a couple of Lieutenant JGs. The sailors on watch at the base of the ramp seemed surprised to see their Captain. It was obvious that they had heard about his troubles and had not been expecting him back, but they managed to snap off crisp salutes and pipe him abroad.

At that moment, it seemed to Mac that the entire ship and its loading operating came to a halt. All eyes were on Phillips as he made his way up the gangway, Mac following at a respectable distance. But she could tell that it was the longest walk of his life.

• • •

Her official orders were to interrogate Captain Joseph Phillips and to keep him under observation and report any attempt at flight. (Though exactly where he would flee once at sea was not spelled out.) Her real orders, the ones she had received from Admiral Chegwidden, were simple: stay at his side. Captain Phillips would need someone in his corner, a confidant, and, if it came to that, a defense lawyer. A friend. That the Navy had decided to return him to his old command while an official hearing was pending spoke volumes about the way the Navy did things. Mac suspected—but did not know for sure—that Chegwidden had argued that none of the other officers had been suspected from command, and that to do so to Phillips at this stage of the investigation would be prejudicial.

As for Mac, Chegwidden knew that he would need someone from outside the ship's company, a neutral power to see that prejudice did not extend to the USS *Mackinac* itself. Sailors could sense when their commander's star was on the wane and could assert their power at his expense in a dozen little ways. By the time the Big Mac returned from its voyage, Phillips would be a lame duck, and possibly a sitting duck as well.

They made the long climb to the bridge, causing a stir among the officers there. There were warm smiles and hearty handshakes from a number of men; among one or two others, there was distinct coolness. There were three new arrivals, men Phillips had not encountered before. One, his new Executive Officer, stepped forward and saluted crisply.

"Lieutenant Commander Greg Haas, sir," he said, his eyes focused somewhere over the captain's right shoulder. He was stone-faced and handsome, somewhere in his late twenties, his youth camouflaged with a fortuitous head of prematurely gray hair. Mac figured him every inch the fast tracker.

"Been waiting for a new XO for sixth months, Hass," said Phillips affably. "Welcome aboard the *Mackinac*."

"It's a pleasure, sir." He saluted again and then took a step back as if he had just been presented with the Navy Cross.

The ship's navigation officer was also new issue. He was a short, stock African American, a full lieutenant named Alton Bennett. He was a little less formal than Haas, but not by much.

Phillips smiled broadly at the third new issue, a rotund man in his mid-forties, a commander jg Naval Reserve. "Danny Fusco!" said Phillips. "What are you doing here? Still playing sailor, huh?"

Fusco grinned. "You ever sold insurance, Captain?"

"No, I haven't."

"This is a lot more fun."

"What are you signed on as?"

"Steering officer, sir."

"Steering?" Phillips looked around the bridge. "Where is Vic? Vic Malone?"

"He's at officer's school in Pensacola, sir," said Haas. "Thought you knew all about it."

"Pensacola, that's right," said Phillips, trying to cover up his ignorance. His power had already been eroded.

There was no hiding Sarah MacKenzie. "Gentlemen, we have Major MacKenzie traveling with us this trip. As you can see, the Major is a Marine, and she is JAG. You are all aware, I know, of the unfortunate event that befell Captain Allan Hawkes last week." Phillips paused for a very long time. "Major MacKenzie is, as you have no doubt gathered, a part of the investigating team. As one of the last people to see Al—that is, Captain Hawkes—alive, I suppose I must be considered a suspect, and therefore liable to investigation." Phillips's voice firmed. "As your commanding officer, I place you under order to show her all courtesies, and you will answer any questions she may have without regard to difference in rank." Phillips's eyes swept the men on the bridge. "Is that clear?"

Like one they answered: "Yes, sir."

"Good. I would appreciate it if you would make this known to the men throughout the ship. XO?"

Haas jumped as if he had been struck by lightning. "Sir!"

"We should have finished loading by now. Get it finished, and when it is, take her to sea."

"Very good, Captain."

"Major MacKenzie . . . If you would come with me. . . ."

Mac followed Phillips down a flight of stairs and stepped into the Captain's Office, a small room just under the bridge. Phillips had, like most Captains, tried to make the spare, gray little room a little more inviting, but despite the few family pictures and the gold leaf port (left) and starboard (right) gag pictures one saw all over the service, the place already felt like a cell.

"They think I did it, too," he said quietly, as if he was confessing to her. For a moment, the woman in her almost overrode the Marine and the JAG officer in her, she wanted to take his hand and tell him things would be all right. But she caught herself.

"It's hard for them, sir," she said. "It's harder for you than for them, but they've never been confronted with anything like this before. You have to remember that."

Phillips smiled crookedly. "And you have to remember, Major, I've never been confronted with anything like this, either."

Mac half-smiled. "I guess not."

Captain Phillips stretched behind his desk and shook his head, smiling ruefully. "You know, Major . . . I am a family man. I have two kids. Boy and a girl—almost grown up. Hell, they *are* grown up. Both of them are post-doc candidates in college. Matt in history at Stanford, Linda is doing something with Mathematics at Columbia that only God can understand. . . ."

"And your wife?" Mac asked.

"She's in real estate," said Phillips. He sounded as if there was something faintly disreputable about real estate.

"You know," said Phillips, "I'm just an ordinary guy. A man. I like beer, football, the Republican party, the Episcopalian church. The Dodgers. I've killed a lot of people . . . for the Navy. In Vietnam, in Desert Storm, and all the little wars in between—Grenada, Panama—but I would never have killed a fellow officer. A brother. A friend . . . The Navy gets that part of me. Other things I keep separate. But God help me, I love the Navy.''

In the deep lines of Captain Phillips's face, she could see that leaving the Navy might be the worst part of this whole ordeal.

The Big Mac was scheduled for what would be a short cruise. A sail down to the Caribbean for an unloading on the Nimitz, which was currently cruising that blue sea awaiting a lengthier deployment to the South Atlantic. That would be followed by a pickup in Panama, then the run back up the coast to Newport News. In all, a nice easy seven-day run. Mac would be on board for the entire trip, and beyond—those were Chegwidden's orders, and she intended to stick to them.

After getting settled in her quarters, Sarah MacKenzie set out to explore this odd ship. The USS *Mackinac* was big and old, but it was probably the cleanest ship Mac had ever been on. There was not a spot bare of paint, a smear of grease, or even the faintest hint of corrosion anywhere. Every bolt had been tightened, every door that should be locked was locked—there wasn't even a burned-out lightbulb. So while the Big Mac may have been the ugliest ship in the Navy, it was almost the most shipshape she had ever been on.

They were underway now, the big boat being cinched out of its berth by three tugs. Soon they would be on the open sea. Mac went below the mid-deck and descended further into the bowels of the ship. The ship seemed as deep as it was long, and it was more than just a supply ship; it was a floating repair station, as well. There were acres of machine shops and power plants, with sailors working over machines that would have been more at home on a factory floor than on a ship.

She paused to watch a sailor in an electronic shop as he worked over a piece of circuitry with a soldering iron. Although intent on what he was, he became aware of her presence and looked up, pushing the Plexiglas shield from his face.

"Can I help you, Major?"

"I just wondered what you were doing?"

The young man smiled. "They say we're going to resupply the Nimitz, ma'am—down here we could *build* the Nimitz."

Mac laughed. "No, really . . ."

The sailor put down his tools. "If we show up and they say they need such and such a circuit board, we'll make it to order."

Mac nodded and walked on. The Ugliest Ship in the Navy they called it, but no one seemed to have a chip on their shoulder about serving on it. No one she had met so far, anyway. They seemed proud to be here, doing work essential to the well-being of the United States Navy. Maybe it wasn't as glamorous as flying jets or driving a Trident, but no one seemed to think of themselves as second-class citizens.

In Mac's experience, a ship reflected the personality of the Captain, and the USS *Mackinac* was tight, not taut; well-run, but not pointlessly spit and polish. It was beginning to seem similar to the way she would describe Captain Joe Phillips. Suddenly, down there, in the bowels of that vast ship, Sarah MacKenzie began to have the feeling that suspect number one was being set up. . . .

eight ✈

SOMEWHERE IN THE PERSIAN GULF

IF IT WAS HOT IN THE AMERICAN NORTH-
east, it was unusually cool in the Middle East, a bless-
edly cool night in the Straits of Hormuz. In the
autumn, the winds normally carry hot air off the
southern desert plains of Yemen, across the narrow
opening of the Persian Gulf and beyond into Iran.

But that night, the winds were from the north and
the mist and the chill in the air made the temperatures
dip well into the mid-fifties. Looking back on it, the
unusual weather would have been interpreted as a bad
omen.

The Heavy Crude Carrier Athgos-Petrotrade was a
Liberian-flagged tanker, Greek owned, but whose of-

fices were registered in the Cayman Islands. The crew was almost exclusively Filipino, with two Chinese officers and a Norwegian Captain, Olaf Tanskannen, known around the world as "Lucky Olaf."

Tanskannen was an old hand at sailing the Gulf. He regularly hauled more crude oil out of the Arabian lake in a year than most masters did in five. He was a capable seaman, affable, but fearless—he was one of the few who made his way through those tricky waters hauling crude even during the war between Iran and Iraq, when the Straits had been little more than a shooting gallery littered with military and civilian wrecks.

It was during that spell that he had gotten his nickname—and he *did* consider himself lucky, so much so that he was convinced that no ship under his command would ever hit a mine; face an aerial attack; or run aground, tear her bottom out, and sink.

For more than twenty-five years, Lucky Olaf had been right. That string of luck would run out that chilly night.

The toughest part of transiting the Straits of Hormuz came in maneuvering through the section known as the Qawerty Shoals. Depending on the flow of the tide, the shoals could be the size of a largish island or mere pinpricks like teeth rising above the greenish waters of the gulf. Either way, it took careful steering and a constant updating of the wind and tides to make it through this, the narrowest part of a very narrow strait.

The Athgos-Petrotrade was sailing easy that night.

The sea was calm, the winds, though chilly, were gusting, but only at 10 knots. Tanskannen was on the bridge watching the slow and steady progress of his ship as it made its way south. The vessel was loaded to the gunwales with Kuwaiti oil. Thick and sweet, with the consistency of peanut butter, the Athgos-Petrotrade had eleven thousand tons of the stuff in her tanks, bound for refineries in Rotterdam's oil terminal Europort.

Tanskannen was on the bridge, breathing a little easier now that the Athgos-Petrotrade had made her way through the worst of the shoals, when his eyes were pulled off the control panel for a moment. There was a sudden flash of light off to the east. At first he thought it was the stem of a refinery stack suddenly coming to life, but it lasted too long—and it was growing bigger.

Tanskannen studied the red-and-orange ball of flame for a moment. It was not all that unusual for this part of the world—so much oil and gas was being pumped out of the ground around here that the air was filled with fumes and effluence. From time to time when they erupted, they were known as "foofs" or "foofies," and were commonly mistaken by the uninitiated for UFOs.

But this ball of flame was too big to be a foof, and besides, it was moving. In fact, Tanskannen had the uncomfortable feeling that it was headed toward him. Instinctively, he fell on the alarm button on the control console. The Klaxon blared once, then the first Silkworm missile struck the tanker dead amidships.

• • •

They felt the blast thirty miles away in Oman. The British Naval Base at Ghorta was the first to respond. A Lynx helicopter with night vision capability was launched to investigate, though by the time the chopper arrived at the sight of the wreck, there was no need for any NV equipment. The Athgos-Petrotrade had broken into three huge chunks, which burned in the middle of a lake of fiery oil like wicks in a candle. Each of the Silkworms carried a warhead containing seven hundred and fifty pounds of explosives, and the three explosions had proven powerful enough to ignite the thick crude. The oil was floating on the water, burning for a radius of three miles, burning waves slapping against the rocks of the shoals.

The Lynx circled, but could not get close enough to the inferno to look for survivors, though each member of the four-man chopper crew knew that any search would be futile. Olaf Tanskannen and his crew had vaporized seconds after the first missile had hit.

The sinking of the Athgos-Petrotrade sent shock waves around the world.

The CIA and the intelligence agencies of a dozen other countries quickly determined that the missiles had been fired from Qusham Alaq, a tiny dot of an island about two miles off the coast of southern Iran. Further intelligence determined that the weapons had been launched by a militant group of Iranian soldiers, known as the Qobo. They were extreme in an extremist country, and believed that the Persian Gulf belonged to Persia, that is to say, Iran. The Qobo, in addition, were still fighting the Iran–Iraq war, and taking out a tanker filled with some of the small amount of Iraqi oil that was allowed to be sold was considered a very hard kick in Saddam Hussein's pants.

But there were other, more ominous implications of this disaster. As the Athgos-Petrotrade continued to burn, fax machines all over the Middle East and Europe were receiving a series of demands—the Qobos wanted *all* the money received from the sale of "their" oil. They made it clear that the Straits of Hormuz was effectively blocked, and also pointedly mentioned that they had Silkworms by the score, some of which were loaded with poisonous gas. They would fire on any ship that attempted to remove the wreckage of the Athgos-Petrotrade or put out the fire.

Thus, in a matter of seconds, there was a crisis in the Gulf.

The USS *Mackinac* was 150 miles off the coast of Miami when word of the sinking first arrived. The news came not by radio or fax, but in the form of a speedy SeaHawk helicopter heading for the Big Mac at top speed.

Captain Phillips and Mac had been on the bridge when the Communications Officer on the SeaHawk called in requesting permission to land to put on a "Special Emissary" from Atlantic Naval Operations Command.

"What the hell is this all about?" Phillips wondered aloud.

The appearance of the helicopter broke the monotony of the hot, sultry morning. Mac followed Phillips off the bridge, down to the main deck, and back toward the helicopter pad in the stern. The SeaHawk was just setting down when they arrived. The helo touched down with a thump and no sooner was it settled when the side door flew open and the "Special Emissary" stepped out.

Mac couldn't stop herself from breaking out in a wide grin. The Special Emissary was Harmon Rabb.

Ten minutes later, the three of them were sitting in the tiny combat control room of the Mac, a pair of Marines posted outside the door. The cluttered cabin was filled with video displays and the controls of the few weapons that the Big Mac carried, and was the most secure room on the ship.

Harm got down to business quickly, telling them about the sudden flare-up in the Gulf, a story that was only now being released to the general media.

"That's terrible," said Phillips. "No wants another Gulf War."

"It could happen, sir," said Harm soberly.

"But I don't get it," said Mac. "What has this got to do with you, Harm? Why have you been sent here? Not that I'm not happy to see you, or anything. . . ."

"Its not about me," said Harm. "It's about Captain Phillips. The President is dispatching all available naval assets to the region. And that means carriers—and that means the USS *Eisenhower*."

"Really?" said Phillips. He peered hard at Harm. "What does that mean?"

"The problem is, the *Eisenhower* does not have an experienced Captain on board. And she's due to pull out in less that three hours."

Mac glanced quickly at Phillips. "You mean . . ."

"Navy Ops is in a tight fix and the President wants all the big boats out now." He turned to Phillips. "Captain, I am here to pass on a message directly from Naval Ops," he said. "You are expected to board the USS *Eisenhower* by 0900 hours, to take over all operations and sail at speed to the Persian Gulf."

Phillips paled. "Oh God . . . I didn't want to get one this way."

"It's nothing to worry about, sir," said Harm. "The Navy is sending you where they want you, and right now they want you to command the *Eisenhower*."

"I hope I can handle it," said Phillips.

"Navy Ops thinks you can, sir," Harm said. "And I suggest we get moving. The Ike has to leave as soon as possible."

"We?" asked Phillips.

Harm nodded. "Yes. The Inquiry is going to be held en route. They'll be flying the principals aboard as we head for the Gulf. So Mac and I have to go along, too."

"What as? My baby-sitters?"

Harm shook his head. "No, sir. We're your lawyers."

nine ✈

THE TUGS WERE ALREADY PUSHING THE
USS *Eisenhower* out of its berth by the time the
SeaHawk helo reached Newport News. Even from
three thousand feet, the carrier looked immense.
Though the three passengers in the SeaHawk had seen
carriers before—in fact, Harm and Phillips had flown
fighters off of them—the reality of such a huge ship
always came as a shock, no matter how many times
they saw one. It was so huge and stood so tall off the
water, that the ship's ability to float seemed to defy
some basic law of physics.

The *Eisenhower* displaced 82,000 tons, the deck
was more than a thousand feet long. It carried 230
combat aircraft—an air force larger than that of some
countries—and held below decks conventional and

nuclear weapons which contained more destructive fire than all the bombs dropped in the twentieth century by all sides, combined.

More than 5,000 sailors called the Ike home. Half of the company ran the ship—the reactors, the steam launching catapults, the weapon systems—while the other half flew and maintained the aircraft. The Ike had seen action, big and small, from the Gulf War to relief efforts in Haiti and Somalia, to police actions in the Adriatic facing Bosnia. Now the big carrier seemed to be off to war again.

The ship was so huge that the landing of the smallish SeaHawk helo on the acres of its deck went almost unnoticed. The helo set down just aft of the carrier island, the nerve center of the ship that looked like a small, gray office building set down on the starboard side of the vessel; and Harm, Phillips and Mac jumped out quickly. The helo crewmen tossed their luggage after them, then the pilot gunned his engines and the SeaHawk was up and off again.

An officer was waiting for them, crouched down to avoid the swash from the helo as he scurried forward.

"Glad to have you aboard, sir," he yelled, fighting with the engine noise to make himself heard. "Lieutenant Commander Mike Kumagai."

Captain Phillips shook hands with the young Asian-American officer. "Thanks, Commander."

"I'm the intelligence officer, sir." He could speak in a more normal tone of voice as the SeaHawk backed off. "Naval Ops thought I should show you around." He turned and signaled to someone way up on the flight bridge. Suddenly the intercom was squealing, piping the Commander aboard, which was immediately followed by a stern announcement: "The Captain is aboard the ship . . ."

Everything, everywhere stopped for a second as Phillips saluted the bridge. Harm watched the veteran Naval Officer as this little ceremony was played out. There were tears in Phillips's eyes.

"He finally got what he wanted," Harm whispered to Mac. "He just never thought he would get it this way."

"That's how life is," Mac replied. "You take a lot of strikes before you hit that home run."

Harm looked surprised and amused. "You never told me you were a baseball fan, Mac."

"There's lots you don't know about me," she said with a sweet smile.

Kumagai took them inside the island and led them up to the Captain's Quarters (CQ). As they made their way through the ship, every head turned to catch a glimpse of the new Old Man. If a cloud of suspicion somehow hung over him, he gave no sign, but he walked uncertainly into the CQ, the sanctum of his old friend Allan Hawkes. The late Captain's personal effects had been removed, but Phillips looked around the spacious quarters with a sad look in his eyes.

"Not the first time I've been in here," he said. Then, aware that he had a job to do, he straightened up and squared his shoulders. "Commander Kumagai?"

"Sir!"

"I want the XO and the CAG in the CIC in five."

"Yessir!"

"And show Commander Rabb and Major Mac-Kenzie to their quarters."

"Yes, sir."

They left him in the care of two Marines—the Ike had no less than thirty-five Marines on board to keep an eye on the weapons stores and perform security duties. Two were always on hand wherever the Captain of the carrier moved about his ship. This had nothing to do with Phillips's present predicament—rather, it was standard operating procedure that the commander of the vessel always had bodyguards.

Harm and Mac found their quarters on the second level, where visiting officers were always housed. They were installed at the end of a long passageway in rooms adjacent to one another.

"Gee, no doorway connecting us," Harm said playfully. "No secret passage between our berths."

"Now why would we need such a thing, Commander?" Mac asked him with a straight face.

Harm gave a good-natured shrug. "You never know when you need a knight in shining armor—you know, someone to come to the rescue of a damsel in distress."

Mac smiled. "Well, Commander Rabb, there are five thousand people on this boat—I'm sure at least 4,500 of them are strong, able-bodied men."

"Yes, so?"

"So, I'm sure if this damsel finds herself in distress," she told him, "there will be no shortage of knights in shining armor."

With that she picked up her bags and walked into her berth, closing the door behind her.

Harm just shook his head. "This will be an interesting voyage," he said aloud. "Very interesting."

They were seven hours out of Newport News when the carrier's air wing came aboard. The ship's major complement of combat aircraft had been ashore when the order to head for the Persian Gulf had come in. As per usual procedure, the planes were kept at a Naval Air Station near Newport News when the carrier was in port. In this case, the air wing had been temporarily staying at Oceania NAS, but now, with a crisis in full bloom in the Gulf, the planes had to get back onto the carrier as quickly as possible.

Harm and Mac joined Phillips on the bridge to watch the landing. It was an awe-inspiring, slightly terrifying procedure to behold. The air wing consisted of three squadrons of F/A-18 Hornet fighter bombers, each squadron containing eighteen planes each. In addition, there were three squadrons of F-14 Tomcat fighters, plus one squadron of absolutely ancient EA-6 Prowlers, electronic warfare aircraft that had been borrowed from a nearby Naval Reserve squadron. There were two more squadrons of planes as well, these craft given over to refueling planes, antisub aircraft, and general transit craft.

You could never get tired of watching an airplane land on a carrier. The first to arrive was an F/A-18 Hornet. The sleek, large airplane doubled as a fighter and a bomber. The lead plane came in low over the stern, its engines screaming as the pilot tried to juggle the million details of the landing. It was a delicate dance: maintaining correct airspeed, matching the speed of the plane to the speed of the boat, watching the wind direction and the pitch of the ship. The Hornet slammed down onto the carrier deck, snagging the number two arresting cable with a hideous scream of hot metal. The pilot immediately throttled up in case the snag was not a good one. But once caught, he just as quickly throttled back down, again filling the deck with an ear-splitting screech. A slam, a bang, and the plane was down.

From approximately 120 miles an hour to zero in less than two seconds. "Like having sex in a car wreck," was how more than one naval aviator had described the experience.

Of course, Harm knew all about this kind of thing—he used to do it for a living—until that night long ago when he almost killed himself during a daring landing, which was followed by the discovery of a severe case of night blindness, and thus restricted him from flight duty. "The Navy gave me an airplane and when I broke it they wouldn't give me another one," he would say ruefully.

Now, as the next plane bounced in, followed by the next and the next, Mac couldn't help but see the sad look on Harm's face. It was as if each plane that bounced in drove a little nail into his heart. She knew he was a brave man, talented, smart, able—maybe even fearless. And she knew that probably nothing bothered him more than the fact that the thing he loved doing best—flying Navy jets off aircraft carriers—was lost to him, probably forever.

Yet still, in those sad eyes, she could see the faint glimmer of hope. With each plane that banged in, it grew. It was so easy to read—as easy as his pain. Maybe, he was thinking, maybe one day. Someday, he would be able to do that again. . . .

It took just ninety minutes for the entire air wing to get down, an astonishingly brief time considering the fact that there were hundreds of airplanes banging in. And yet, it was absolutely routine—due completely to the skill of the pilots and the high level of training of the carrier's deck crew.

Harm and Mac watched the entire spectacle while Phillips ran the ship like a pro. Everyone treated him as he should have been treated: like the commander of the largest ship in the U.S. fleet, heading for war. There was hardly any sign that this man was the number one suspect in the murder of the carrier's previous commander—certainly not from Phillips himself. He seemed to have managed to put the accusation behind him—after all, he was too busy to think about anything else. If an observer had not known those gruesome circumstances, he or she would have thought that all was normal on the bridge—as normal as things could be, considering where the carrier was going and why.

Once the air wing was aboard, Phillips ordered the *Eisenhower* to full speed. The result was immediate, as if someone down below had pushed a stick shift into fifth gear and stomped down hard on an accelerator. The huge boat lurched ahead with a discernible thump, and inside of sixty seconds, they were traveling very fast through the choppy Atlantic waters.

• • •

Harm and Mac shared a cup of coffee in the officers' mess, then took a stroll out onto the suddenly quiet deck. With the air wing aboard and safely tucked away below, the primary thing to do now was to get across the Atlantic, through the Suez Canal and into the Straits of Hormuz as quickly as possible. They walked to the stern of the ship and looked back at the wide, roiling wake.

"I've been on speedboats that haven't gone this fast," said Mac. "Just how fast are we going?"

Harm winked. "Top-secret fast."

Both of them, however, were aware that they were not along for a joyride. Their conversation turned to the inquiry.

"Isn't it kind of strange to have this inquiry on a ship underway?" Mac asked. "What's the hurry?"

"The Ike needs a commander—if not Phillips, then someone else. He's got to be cleared or charged as soon as possible." Harm turned, leaned his back against the railing, and looked up to the bridge. "Besides, you don't know your Naval history, Major. Boards of inquiries and even courts-martial have been held on the high seas before; it's been going on for centuries. Back in the days of sail, a ship might be out for two years. Any trouble would have to be dealt with. Couldn't wait till they got home."

"Thanks for the history lesson," said Mac acidly. "Still, you can't deny that this is unusual."

Harm nodded. "Unusual is a nice way of putting it. The location of the court doesn't make it any less serious."

"The board is going to have to determine whether

there is enough evidence to press formal charges against Captain Phillips for the death of Captain Hawkes.'' Mac paused a moment. ''But my question is—where's the board?''

''There will be six officers,'' Harm explained. ''Three from the *Eisenhower* and three from the rest of the carrier group.'' Both of them scanned the horizon for the flotilla of ships that traveled with every carrier. They could see no other ship; the sea was completely empty. ''Well, they're out there somewhere.''

''There will be a prosecutor . . . any idea who they're sending?''

''No idea,'' said Harm. ''But I've found out who the judge is . . . it's the Bull himself.''

''Oh boy,'' said Mac.

Admiral Ambrose T. ''Bull'' Selden was something of a legend around JAG. He had started life as a Navy flier in Vietnam, then commanded an Aegis cruiser. Then, to everyone's surprise, he left command to attend Harvard Law School. From there he went into JAG and nailed every case he prosecuted. Now he was a judge. He was known as ''tough but fair,'' which was okay, but defense attorneys preferred it the other way around—put the fair part first and let the tough part bring up the rear.

''So this is what we do,'' Harm said. ''Divide and conquer. I'll emphasize the questioning of the principals involved. Conroy, McKitrick, and Mattingly will be coming aboard, and I'll take them through their stories. Mac, you have the background on these guys and we have to find the ammo that will point the finger away from Phillips and, we hope, toward one of the others."

"I saw Phillips at work on the Big Mac, Harm. He's a great Captain and he was proud of that ship. He ran it like it was the pride of the fleet. I know he would never kill to get a better command."

"Knowing isn't proof . . . but you have to wonder why Hawkes was promoted ahead of him," Harm mused. "I mean, there is a certain amount of politics involved in any promotion, particularly a big one like that. But when push comes to shove, the Navy usually selects the most qualified person for the job based on past performance, not on politics."

Mac shrugged. "The *Mackinac* was the ugliest ship I've ever seen, but the crew certainly made the best of it. They were efficient, they were proud . . . and it came from the top down."

"Now all we have to do is prove him innocent," said Harm "Any ideas?"

"Not yet. You?"

"Yes."

"What?"

"I think we have to unleash our secret weapon," said Harm.

Mac looked puzzled. "I didn't know we have a secret weapon. Do we have a secret weapon?" she asked. "What is it?"

"It's not a what. It's a who."

"Who?" Mac asked dutifully.

Harm smiled. "Why, Bud Roberts, of course."

ten ✈

BUD ROBERTS WAS ALONE. HE WAS IN A field, a field he knew to be located exactly 22.3 miles southeast of JAG Headquarters in Falls Church. There was no other human within at least four thousand feet of him, in any direction. The center of the field was practically treeless, but its borders were formed by an almost-perfect ring of pine trees, cutting the isolated field off from view. It was the perfect place for Bud Roberts. He was, literally, in the middle of nowhere.

Bud Roberts was Harmon Rabb's gofer. Officially his title was Legal Assistant, which carried the rank of ensign, but that didn't begin to tell the story of the scope of his duties. In addition to doing everything a legal assistant would normally do, Bud had done some more unorthodox duties: he had flown in a shot-

109

to-hell supersonic jet; he had baby-sat a rooster on one memorable occasion; he had sat up for three days and nights straight waiting for a phone call that never came, on Harm's orders.

Roberts had volunteered for his position, and over the months had had ample opportunity to ponder that bedrock rule of the military: "Never volunteer for anything."

Today, though, out in that field, he was on his own time, doing something he had been planning for some time. Bud Roberts was flying a kite. Of course, it wasn't just any old kite, but a massive kite with a wingspan of six feet by ten. Its crooked wings gave it a faintly menacing air, making it look like some kind of flying dinosaur—a pterodactyl, perhaps. The kite had a small black box affixed to its spine, right at the point where the cross struts met. That box was crammed with electronic bits and pieces that Bud had carefully soldered together.

The line by which Bud controlled the kite was no ordinary piece of twine, either. Rather, it was a series of think wires, each wrapped in lightweight electrical tape, then braided together to create a relatively light-weight cord. Signals were now running down some of those wires even as a slight but steady stream of electricity was running up others, those attached to a battery pack that Bud had set up nearby.

This whole setup was the prototype of an invention that Bud Roberts had been thinking about for some time. This kite, then, was obviously no ordinary kite; it was a weapon of war. Bud Roberts had considered a problem, and he thought he had found a solution.

Suppose a SEAL team or any other kind of special ops soldiers were behind enemy lines, their job to call a smart-bomb strike on an enemy target. Smart bombs can now be directed by the Global Positioning System (GPS). But while a field team might have a GPS module locating its position, the attacking plane would have to know the target's GPS position for a laser-guided air strike.

Bud's solution: send a small GPS console up in a kite, steer it over the target, and let the bombs rain down. Just like that . . .

But even the greatest inventor runs into trouble now and then. And Bud had his hands full. The kite was flying, but it was totally out of control. Spinning, dipping, diving wildly with Bud at the other end of the wires, the kite seemed to be intent on shaking him off, the way a horse will try and scrape its rider off under a low branch. Bud ran forward, he ran backward, he ran in a series of ever-widening circles. For a single terrifying second, his feet left the ground, as if the kite was going to carry him off like a bird of prey. He was fighting desperately to prevent the kite from crashing to the ground and pulverizing the couple of hundred bucks' worth of Bud's gadgetry in the black box, not to mention the GPS locator he had borrowed from a buddy at the Annapolis weapons training ground.

He'd been fighting this battle against the wind for about ten minutes, trying like crazy to get the kite and its package stabilized. He pretty much had it now, but he was panting from the exertion, his arms hurt, and there was an ache in the back of his neck as he stared up at his wind-borne contraption.

"There," he gasped. "That should do it." Then the kite hit a pocket of dead air and plummeted to the ground like a grouse that had just been bagged. It seemed that the sound of tearing and cracking was as loud as a thunderclap.

Then Bud's cell phone began to ring. Bud was furious with himself and with whoever was calling at that inopportune moment. It was all Bud could do to prevent himself from taking a bite out of the phone instead of answering it.

"Hello?" he snapped. Bud Roberts was almost unfailingly polite.

The person on the other end hesitated a moment, taken aback by the snarl. Then Bud heard a voice he recognized. "Hey, Bud. Did I get you at a bad time?" Harmon Rabb asked.

"No, sir," Roberts almost screamed. "I mean, yes sir. I mean . . . where the heck are you, sir?"

"That's classified," Harm replied. "But I'm calling you with a big assignment. This one is important."

Bud was walking across the grass to the crash site. The kite, the GPS console, and the black box were all a total wreck.

"Go ahead," said Bud, his shoulders slumping. "Whatever you want, sir."

"Bud, I'm going to ask you to dig deep into some of the most boring information imaginable," Harm told him. "Normally, it might have taken you days to dig out the information I need. But you don't have that much time . . . All I can promise you is that the Navy will reimburse you for all the coffee you're going to drink.''

''Sounds . . . well, interesting, sir,'' Bud said, toeing among the remains of the very expensive, very bent and twisted GPS module.

''Interesting it will not be,'' Harm told him. ''But important, yes.''

''How's that, sir?''

''Important enough to save a man's life,'' Harm told him.

And that's when Bud suddenly began paying attention. ''Captain Phillips, sir?'' he asked Harm, even though it was probably against a million rules of protocol.

''That too is top secret,'' Harm replied. ''But you're a good guesser. Can you do it? Do you have time? Or has Admiral Chegwidden got you juggling everything in the air while we're gone?''

''No, sir, no problem,'' he said. ''Everything I got is firmly on the ground.'' But he didn't know whether to laugh or cry at this final remark.

eleven

THE MID-ATLANTIC STORM BLEW UP quickly, but no one was surprised by it. The weather officer on the *Eisenhower* had been monitoring conditions for hours, and he could see all the elements coming together. It was a common enough occurrence in the middle of the cold Atlantic as winter came on— fierce tropical depressions, the ones that couldn't quite make it across to the Caribbean, formed near hurricanes in the middle of the Atlantic instead and were strong enough to blow anything that floated all over the ocean. The Ike, weighing 90,000 tons, was a good example of how powerful nature could be— the big carrier was rocking and rolling like a water ride at an amusement park.

The rocking had been going on for seven hours

straight, and enough rain had fallen on the *Eisenhower*'s decks to drown a small city. But the carrier had been in much worse weather and it ploughed on, battering its way through towering waves and tough headwinds while the members of the crew went about their tasks as if they were experiencing nothing more than a light spring shower.

Planes were launched, planes were recovered. The carrier never went anywhere unless a few F-14s were in the air watching over it. A fifty-knot gale and a drenching mid-ocean rain could not change that. It made launching and landing that much more interesting. However, it could get a little rough for non-crew members who weren't used to such "interesting" weather.

The principals in the board of inquiry had been due aboard the Ike at 1430 hours. It was now 1435. Harm and Mac were on the bridge, scanning the horizon for any sign of the long-range C-2C Greyhound transit plane. Radio contacts with the C-2C had been intermittent over the last hour and a half; there had been nothing but silence and static for the last twenty minutes. This didn't mean that the airplane had crashed—not yet, anyway. But if they didn't hear from it soon, then Harm would begin to worry that something had happened to it.

The C-2C Greyhound was the plane usually used for carrier-hopping, the Navy's version of an air taxi. The plane was rugged and could take this weather for a good long period of time—but it couldn't take it forever. The Ike was a big boat, but the ocean was bigger and it was possible to get lost in weather like this. If the C-2C got lost, there was the real possibility that it would run low on fuel. Air-sea rescues are tricky at the best of times, under the best of conditions—Harm hoped and prayed that there wouldn't be one that gray afternoon.

Tension increased on the bridge; it could be felt rising like humidity. Phillips was getting concerned as the seconds ticked away and there was still no sign of the Greyhound. Harm looked at him as the Captain looked at his wristwatch for the fourth time in under fifteen seconds, and wondered what thoughts must be going through his head. If the C-2 went down, then three people who could prove his guilt or innocence would be lost forever. What did that mean, exactly? Would Phillips feel free and clear, as if he had gotten away with the perfect crime? Or would he be doomed to doubt and guilt for the rest of his life, forced to ignore the whispers that would follow him through the rest of his career?

Harm knew something that Joseph Phillips did not. If there was no court of inquiry—even if charges were never filed—the Captain's career was effectively over. Sure, the Navy would keep him on the Ike until this crisis in the Middle East was over, but without an official hearing and an ironclad proof of innocence, Phillips was done for. He could win World War Three single-handedly and it would not make one bit of difference.

Either flying jets off a carrier or arguing a case as a JAG officer, Harm Rabb had learned that there was no room for ambiguity in the U.S. Navy. Phillips needed a spotless record or he had no record at all;

let the slightest trace of tarnish remain, and he was as dead as Hawkes himself: "You remember Joe Phillips. They were going to nail him for the death of Allen Hawkes, until all the witnesses got killed. Convenient, huh?"

At that moment, the bridge radio crackled to life. "I got a radio signal, sir!" the radio operator clutched the headphones close to his ears.

"The C-2?" Phillips asked.

"No sir, an F-14. But not one of ours." The communications operator looked puzzled.

"Pipe it into the intercom so we can all hear it," Phillips ordered.

"CVN-69, this is F-14 Tango Green. Do you read? Over." No one recognized the designation or the voice.

Phillips nodded to the comm officer. "Answer."

"We read you, Tango Green."

"Ambrose Selden here, CVN-69. I've got a stray tailing me. A C-2. They seem to have trouble with their radio. Can you light your beacon and make it hot, please? I'm gonna let that stray come in before me, they seem to be having a little fuel problem. Is that okay?"

"Jesus Christ!" said the comm. "It's Bull Selden!" The comm looked awfully embarrassed. The tension on the bridge was broken immediately, Joe Phillips laughing the loudest.

"A man whose given name is Ambrose and whose nickname is Bull—and who chooses to use Ambrose." Phillips laughed some more and shook his head slowly. "Someone do as the Admiral asks and turn on the homing beacon to full power."

Not thirty seconds had passed before the C-2 burst out of the clouds and slammed down on to the pitching, rain-slick deck of the carrier. There was a screech, a crunch, a bump, and a bang, but the airplane managed a good trap and was down, safe at a standstill in two seconds.

The plane was hastily directed to the parking stand at the side of the deck. No sooner had it come to a halt when the rear door opened and three men got out. Even from the distance of the bridge, Phillips, Harm, and Mac could see them clearly. It was Mattingly, McKitrick, and Conroy. Both Harm and Mac looked over at Phillips as the three men were escorted out of the pounding rain. They were his friends, his colleagues, his old classmates—and the three men who might have enough evidence to convict him of murder.

Now another aircraft was coming in. It was the F-14 Tango Green. It banged aboard with a huge, almost painful screeching of wheels and screaming engines. It snagged the two wire and was dragged to a halt. There was a split second burst of fire and power as the pilot killed the two mighty jet engines.

The F-14 was immediately surrounded by the ground crew and the canopy popped open. Ambrose Selden stood up in the cockpit and stretched, as if he had been stuck in traffic during a long suburban commute. He hopped out of his fighter as if he was getting out of a minivan, and took a walk around his aircraft—the post-flight walkaround, just as the book dictated—to make sure that no damage had been done during the flight. A little wind and rain didn't bother him a bit.

"Wow, he really is Superman," said Mac.

"He's got everything except the cape," said Harm, reaching for the binoculars.

More interesting to Harmon was the man who had traveled in the backseat of the Admiral's personal jet fighter.

"Well, I'll be damned," said Harm, the glasses still pressed to his eyes. "If it isn't our old friend George Burgess. . . ."

Burgess was, like Harmon, a Lieutenant Commander JAG. He was a prosecutor of considerable ability. He had been at the Academy a year behind Harmon, had edited the Law Review at Columbia, and knew every trick in the legal book. And sometimes, he would fight dirty. "Now we know who we're up against. I should have guessed."

"Oh hell," said Mac. "Burgess . . ."

Mac and Harm looked at one another. They had seen the future, and the future was bleak.

Though the entire world was focused on the Straits of Hormuz and the vast gathering of forces that was heading to the region, the area immediately surrounding that where the Athgos-Petrotrade had gone down was eerily still and quiet.

Wreckage was still strewn across the water and patches of thick oil burned here and there, but no salvage operations had begun, neither had there been a search for survivors—everyone knew that there weren't any. No one wanted to see if the extremist Iranian group would make good on its threat to blast any ship attempting to enter the area. Everyone was waiting for the cavalry to arrive.

The force steaming toward the Gulf was massive and international, although the U.S. Navy was leading the charge. The coalition that had been put together during Desert Storm had never been dissolved, and troops from a dozen different countries were pouring into Saudi Arabia. There was a certain amount of rhetoric in the United Nations about the encroachment of foreign troops in that part of the world, but no one was listening to the Ambassadors from the weaker, more militant states; this time even Iraq was quietly acknowledged to be on the right side of the conflict, for once—though no one said it that way publicly (except for the commentators on NPR, National Public Radio).

No one—not even NPR—reported the statements coming out of the Iranian government. These communiqués were deeply secret and not released to the media, but the Foreign Office in Teheran was telling any government that would listen that it was at a loss about what to do with the Qobos—the subtext was that they were fearful about doing anything at all, for fear that a couple of Silkworms filled with the anthrax virus would fall on Teheran and Qom.

But the straits themselves were quiet. No ships were passing through them, of course; there was no ship within a hundred miles of where Lucky Olaf's luck had run out. From time to time, a British Army helicopter would dash through those dangerous skies, checking to see if the other side had made any more threatening moves.

Nothing had happened. The Qobos were quiet. The water burned. But everyone knew that a war could erupt in this confined space at any moment. The smallest incident could ignite the entire region.

And that incident began with one of those British Lynx choppers sent out on armed recon patrol. It was one hour out of its base in Oman when it came upon a small fleet of gunboats moving away from mainland Iran. There were twenty of them in all, all the same type and size, each armed with a fifty-caliber machine gun and at least a few rocket launchers. The boats were traveling in a long single line, and the helo crew recognized that formation right away—it was a typical mine-sweeping configuration. The militants were now laying mines around the wreckage of the Athgos-Petrotrade, information which was relayed back to Oman quickly and efficiently by the crew on the Lynx.

The ante had been upped. Once the allied force was in place, the first of their countermoves would be to send salvage crews into the area in an attempt to clear the Straits for the eventual resumption of shipping traffic. The salvage ships—powerful ocean-going tug-boats—carried no weapons and had to hope that the military force behind it would protect them from attack. But no one could protect the big workhorse tugs against mines.

The British helo crew made one last pass over the

flotilla of gunboats, the nose-cone camera transmitting pictures of the scene back to Oman, harvesting as much information as possible for the intelligence analysts who would try to work out a solution to this thorny problem. The camera even picked up the muzzle flashes from one of the boats as one of the fifty cals opened up, firing on the Lynx. A line of shells seemed to stroll along the body of the Lynx, one of them chopping off a piece of the rear stabilizing rotor.

The Lieutenant commanding the chopper felt the machine buck with the impact of the big shells. "Bugger!" He hit the Auto SOS scrambler button on the console in front of him, the automated system immediately broadcasting the chopper's position. Alarms started whining all over the aircraft.

"This is Charlie Foxtrot One . . . We are taking hostile fire. We have been hit. Initiate SAR."

Oman came back immediately. "Received Charlie Foxtrot One. Keep dry, we're on our way."

As the Lynx turned for home, the EWO sitting behind the pilot loosed three TOW missiles, a defensive action to break up the flotilla beneath them. The three lethal weapons slammed homes and almost immediately there were three gunboats on fire and taking water.

The Lynx was out of range of the fifty cals in a matter of seconds, but the first machine-gun barrage was the one that would prove fatal. An oil leak gushed into a broken hydraulic line and the heat from the engine set the oil smoldering. The interior of the helicopter filled with acrid smoke and the pilot felt the controls get slack then seize in his hands. There was no doubt that the aircraft was going down. . . .

The search-and-rescue chopper reached the scene only minutes later, but they found only the smoldering wreckage of the helo floating in the green waters about ten miles from the Omani coast. Divers were dropped into the water, but it was too late. The helo's crew had gone in with their aircraft; all were dead. Four more fatalities in a war that had not even yet begun.

The downing of the Lynx reverberated across the world, having an effect even on Harm Rabb and the Board of Inquiry. News of the latest action reached the USS *Eisenhower* through a message sent to the carrier from Atlantic Central Command. The message was crystal clear: the situation in the Gulf was intensifying, and the Ike had to be on station and "Code One" as fast as possible.

Code One in this case referred directly to the situation on board the USS *Eisenhower*. As far as Naval Command was concerned, the command of the Ike was not as stated "solidified," and that essential piece of war machinery must arrive on station with due haste. There was a second, encrypted communication with this one, directed to Rear Admiral Ambrose Selden, "Eyes Only." If Captain Joseph Phillips was indicted or if the Court of Inquiry had not reached a conclusion in time, then the overall command of the carrier group would go to Selden and the command of the *Eisenhower* would be turned over to the XO.

Harmon Rabb had twenty-four hours to prove Joseph Phillips innocent of a crime.

• • •

124

The room in which the inquiry would be held was the largest cabin on the Ike. Unofficially, it was known as "the Admiral's nest"—the place where an Admiral would stay whenever riding aboard a carrier. In actual fact, it was a dull, cheerless room without windows, with a strip of fluorescent lights and a linoleum floor. In the history of the *Eisenhower*, no Admiral had been known to have stayed there; usually a better cabin would be found for any flag-rank officer elsewhere in the ship. More often than not, the Admiral's nest was used for award ceremonies, staff holiday parties, and larger-than-normal briefings.

There was plenty of room to install a table large enough to accommodate the seven-member court. Facing that were two smaller tables—one for the prosecution and one for the defense. In the middle of the room was a folding chair for the witness.

Both Harm and Mac sighed when they saw the room. It was noisy, ugly, and the lights gave it all the charm of a police interrogation room.

The Inquiry opened at exactly 0800 hours on the morning of their second day at sea. The weather had cleared somewhat during the night, but the *Eisenhower* was still feeling the effects as it slopped and blundered through the deep swells left over by the hurricane.

Harm, Mac, Phillips, and Burgess stood as Selden led the board into the room.

"Please be seated," said Selden. They all sat, Burgess shooting a quick smile over at Harm and a wink at Mac. The wink was a mistake. Mac froze the smug young man with a look so icy that he looked as if he had shrunk slightly.

"Good move," said Harm out of the side of his mouth. "Scare him as often as you can."

Selden checked his watch then gaveled the Board of Inquiry to order. "Before we begin," he said, "I would like to read a message I have just received from Naval Command. The *Eisenhower* is scheduled to be in position within thirty-six hours and whoever is going to command this vessel must have been in command for at least twelve hours. In other words, gentlemen, we have twenty-four hours in which to conclude these proceedings. . . ." He looked around the room. "Commander Burgess, if you would begin please."

"Thank you sir." Burgess did not look flustered anymore, but rather cool and confident. "I would like to start by pointing out to the members of the board that this is not a court of law, that there will be no convictions here. Rather, we are convened to determine whether there is enough evidence to indict Captain Phillips for the murder of Captain Allen Hawkes."

Harm felt Phillips sitting next to him, tense at the mention of the two names. If Phillips was going to go on the witness stand, they were going to have to find a way to calm him down.

"And I think you'll find," Burgess continued, "that there is more than enough evidence to support such an indictment." He proceeded to lay out his evidence, all of it circumstantial but pretty damning, even Harm had to admit that. Phillips had motive, opportunity, proximity to the victim. His judgment was impaired due to alcohol. On those facts alone he recommended that formal murder charges be pressed against Phillips. Burgess's presentation had been quick, concise, and to-the-point, and it made a lot of sense.

Harm had a lot less to work with. His statement was even shorter. Captain Phillips was a professional soldier, a naval officer of the highest character and reputation. There was no reason he would kill a man who had been his friend and colleague for almost thirty years. Harm sat down with a sense that he had not done well by his client.

Selden's face betrayed nothing; he merely banged his gravel. "Commander Burgess," he said, "your first witness, please."

Mattingly was the first person on the docket. He was escorted into the room by a Marine, who walked him to the witness chair.

Mattingly looked miserable and he sat on the very edge of the chair, as if he did not want to lean back, or as if somehow the chair was dirty. Burgess was affable. "Captain, I wonder if you could tell us what happened on the night in question."

Captain Mattingly began to recount the now-familiar details of that fateful October evening.

The five friends had gotten together on the yacht. They ate well, they drank well. They engaged in friendly banter, friendly arguments, none of which ended in rancor. Though fueled by fine wine, fine scotch, and the lethal brew called anchor grease. Voices did become raised on occasion. But this was nothing new, Mattingly pointed out. "We knew each other well enough to argue occasionally," he said simply.

Burgess stepped in to gloss over that possibly exculpatory point. "Once you left the Cats Paw, sir . . . could you tell us what happened?"

Mattingly shifted uncomfortably. "Let's see . . . Admiral McKitrick remained on the yacht. He was going to sail back to Washington that night. The four of us grabbed a cab at the marina and went back to Newport News. I was dropped off first, and everything seemed fine." Mattingly shrugged, as if slightly embarrassed that he didn't have more to offer.

"I see . . ." Burgess walked back to his table, picked up a piece of paper, studied it for a moment, then walked back toward Mattingly. To Harm it looked as if there were only a few lines written on Burgess's pad, the sum total of his notes numbering under a hundred words. Burgess was positive that he could nail Phillips without breaking into a sweat.

"Captain Mattingly," said Burgess, "You have stated that there were disagreements around the dinner table that night."

"Yes."

"And which two men argued loudest and hardest that night?"

"Well," said Mattingly, uncertainly, "it wasn't a knock-down drag-out argument, Commander. It was more that—"

Burgess turned to Selden. "Sir? Could you direct the witness to answer?"

"Answer the question, please Captain."

128

"Could I hear it again?" said Mattingly, desperately stalling. He did not think that Phillips had killed Hawkes, but he knew that his words were not going to help much.

"Let me put it another way," said Burgess affably. "Did Captain Phillips and Captain Hawkes discuss with a degree of passion a certain subject that evening?"

Mattingly seemed to twist in the seat. "Yes, they did."

"And what was that?"

"They argued about the command of the *Eisenhower*," said Mattingly miserably.

"And if Captain Hawkes had not been in command of the *Eisenhower*, who, according to precedent, would have been the next Commander of this great ship?"

"Captain Phillips."

"I see . . . and then did Captain Phillips propose a toast?"

"Yes," said Mattingly.

"And was it a toast to the ill-health and early demise of a serving officer of the U.S. Navy?"

Mattingly almost whispered. "Yes. It was."

Burgess smiled brightly. "Thank you, Captain. No further questions."

Selden looked over at Rabb. "Commander Rabb, your witness."

Harm popped to his feet. "Captain Mattingly . . . who did Captain Phillips propose the toast to?"

"Captain Honneger of the USS *Lexington*."

"And did he do it in jest?"

Mattingly looked very relieved. "Absolutely!"

"And, as far as you know, is Captain Honneger alive and well this morning?"

There was a chuckle from Admiral Selden. "Charlie Honneger is going to live forever," he said.

"That was the unanimous opinion of the group that night, sir," said Mattingly.

"Then despite this threat, Captain Honneger is still with us, is that correct?" Harm asked.

"I have no evidence to the contrary," said Mattingly.

"I have no further questions, sir."

Colonel Conroy was the next witness called. He gave the same account of the evening as Mattingly had, except that he gave his testimony in longer, more detailed fashion. Much more.

Burgess led him through the night, almost minute by minute. He knew the number of bottles of wine consumed, he even knew the vintage. He knew the age of the scotch consumed and he remembered what cocktails had been served before dinner.

Rock-jawed and impassive and without any hint of emotion, Conroy recounted in detail every topic discussed that night, from the chances of the Washington Redskins to the price of diesel fuel. He knew the exact time the yacht shoved off, the exact time dinner was served, the exact time the stewards cleared the table. Conroy could estimate the speed of the Cats Paw II both upstream and down. He knew exactly what time the yacht tied up, the time it disembarked, what time it left the marina for the long ride home.

Once his long recitation was over and they had reached the cab ride, Burgess paused. "Now, after

Captain Mattingly got out of the cab, who was due to be dropped off next?''

''I was.''

''Did anything happen in that cab *before* you were dropped off?''

Conroy nodded. ''Joe suggested a nightcap.''

''And you declined?''

''Yes.''

''And Captain Hawkes?''

''He declined also.''

''And what was Captain Phillips's reaction to that?''

For the first time, Conroy faltered slightly in his testimony. ''Joe was not happy about it, I guess.''

''What do you mean by that, exactly?''

''He called us a few choice names.'' Conroy smiled crookedly.

''A few choice names,'' said Burgess. ''What does that mean, exactly? Did he swear at you?''

''Yes.''

''Would you characterize his speech as foul and abusive?''

''Objection!'' Harm was on his feet. ''Leading the witness.''

''Sustained,'' said Selden.

''I withdraw the question, Admiral,'' said Burgess smoothly. ''Do you recall anything that Captain Phillips said to Captain Hawkes?''

Conroy nodded. ''He said that Allan didn't have the balls to command the *Eisenhower*.''

Phillips whipped around, looked at Harm, and opened his mouth to say something, but Harm held up his hand; he was following the interrogation closely.

"And how did Captain Hawkes respond?"

For a split second Colonel Conroy, warrior extraordinare, looked scared. "He said that they would never know if Phillips had what it took because . . . of his present command."

"Which was the USS *Mackinac*, is that correct?"

"Yes," said Conroy.

"And how exactly did he characterize the *Mackinac*?" said Burgess. He leaned in hard on the SEAL, completely unafraid of him. "You must recall, Colonel. The board has already been dazzled by your command of memory. What did Captain Hawkes say to Captain Phillips?"

Conroy's shoulders slumped. "He said that they would never know because Captain Phillips would be stuck driving his boat around the world—" The last few words came out in a rush, as if he was anxious to get them out and over with. "—servicing the big boys like a two-dollar whore."

"Like a two-dollar whore?" Burgess repeated. "And what was Captain Phillips's reaction to that?"

"He was very angry," said Conroy.

"How angry, Colonel? Angry enough to kill?"

Harm was on his feet again. "Objection, sir. Presumes to know the state of mind of the accused!"

"Sustained," said Selden.

"I'm sorry, sir," said Burgess blandly. "I withdraw the question." He walked back to his table. "No further questions, sir."

Selden looked to Harm. "Mr. Rabb. Your witness."

Harm tried not to look nonplused. "I have no questions for this witness, your honor."

Wham! The gavel came down as loud as a pistol shot. "There will be a five-minute recess."

As a rule, Lieutenant Commanders in the office of the Judge Advocate General do not talk to Captains of serving naval vessels the way Harmon Rabb spoke to Joseph Phillips afterward. He virtually threw the senior man into an anteroom outside the court and glared at him.

"Just what in hell was that all about, Captain? How the hell can you expect me to defend you if you don't tell me that you had been shooting off your mouth like a Goddamned jackass? Why didn't you tell me about the cab ride? Why didn't you tell me that Hawkes had goaded you like that? You might just think I'm a shit-tail little JAG officer, sir, but right now I am all that stands between you and a very long hitch in the brig. You know that, mister?"

"Harm, for God's sake," cautioned Mac.

But Phillips did not seem put out in the least. "Why didn't I tell you, Commander Rabb? Because it never happened. Conroy was lying."

twelve ✈

BUD ROBERTS WAS SO DEEP IN THE EARTH, he felt as if he would never see the sun or breathe fresh air again. At that moment, he was in the sub-sub-sub-basement of a huge, dark building located on the outskirts of D.C., an old tomb of an edifice known as the Naval Maritime Records Depository. Roberts was beginning to think that nothing—*nothing*—in the history of the U.S. Navy had ever happened since the day the keel of the *Bonhomme Richard* had first touched water that hadn't been written down, recorded in some way.

The depository held tens of thousands of acres of paper, records of every event, no matter how minute in the history of the Navy. The room he was in, a dank, poorly lit chamber was about the size of three or four tennis courts, and it held row upon row of steel shelves which ran from floor to very high ceiling, each shelf packed with file folders that held nothing but ships' manifests. Long, long lists of what American naval vessels had carried from port to port, day in day out for the last one hundred years—there was no other kind of paper in that room but manifests.

Of course, these weren't computer records, nice clear printouts that Bud could decipher easily. No, these were handwritten records that every ship was mandated to provide, from both before and during the computer age. Just as the most modern warship afloat had to make position checks by sextant and only then check the GPS, every vessel had to provide handwritten records of their comings and goings and what they did in-between. Once the pages were filled they were sent to the Naval Maritime Records Depository, filed, and then forgotten—until some fool like Bud Roberts came, descended like a minor into the bowels of the building, and unearthed them.

He was also freezing. The weather in Washington had finally gotten the message and turned cold, but, inexplicably, the air-conditioning was on in the sub-sub-sub-basement and Bud had only his uniform jacket to keep him warm. That jacket was sprinkled with dry dust and his fingers were a mass of paper cuts, the result of turning so many of these handwritten log pages. He was tracking the movements of the USS *Mackinac* over the course of its long and busy career. It made for deathly dull reading.

The Big Mac had served just as its designers had intended. It had carried oil, arms, and other supplies to furnish aircraft carriers while they were underway, its powerful engines bearing the strain of keeping up with the swift-moving carrier while stores and fuel were transferred through oil lines and cargo baskets.

But when the Mac was not racing to keep up with carriers, it was performing the duties of other smaller naval vessels: picking up stuff at one point and depositing it at another. Sailors' uniforms manufactured in Bremerton, Washington were delivered to a port in South Carolina. Gear-grinding equipment picked up in Virginia made its way to Bath, Maine. Engine parts for old Navy aircraft were sold to Portugal and delivered to the Portuguese Navy at the docks at Rota. Furniture and household belongings for transiting sailors returning home after long stints overseas were carried from Portsmouth, England to Portsmouth, New Hampshire.

The Big Mac was a huge floating moving van and delivery truck, and in addition to being the Ugliest Ship in the Navy, it certainly was the most boring. Bud Roberts had been working since early morning, starting in 1997 and working backward, and in the eight hours he had been down there he had come upon nothing odd, nothing even slightly unusual, in the manifests.

But then he reached the records for 1989. And that's when Bud Roberts hit his first home run.

It came in the form of what seemed like just another page of dull entries. In March of 1989, the Big Mac had finished performing a stint of refueling of the USS *Independence* during Pacific maneuvers. Returning to the U.S. for a previously scheduled paint job in San Diego, the ship was diverted to the Pacific side of the Panama Canal, where it picked up a shipment of "lightbulbs and electric fans." Then the ship sailed for San Diego, but instead of getting the paint job, it turned around and headed back to Panama, where it picked up a load of "blankets, screw machinery, and lifeboats."

The *Mackinac* returned to San Diego and offloaded this cargo. But again, instead of being painted, it was off to Panama once more, its third trip in as many weeks. This time it picked up a load of "sulfur packs and canned goods," and then dutifully sailed back to San Diego.

The first thing that Bud noticed about this odd coming and going was that the Mac was going *out* empty and coming *back* with cargo. It was simply a given that a ship like the Mac never sailed without being filled with cargo, every square inch taken up with every kind of supply. For the eight years from 1989 to 1997, Bud Roberts could recite the exact tonnage of cargo carried on every trip; it was always the same—44,808 dry weight tons. But then, in 1982 the number appeared to have dropped; on one Panama run it was down to a mere 16,000 tons—a terrible waste of space on a working boat like the Mac.

The second anomaly concerned that last Panama–San Diego run. There was no record of the ship ever loading its cargo in Southern California, or anywhere else, for that matter. Instead, according to the logs, it just sat in San Diego harbor for two full weeks, unloaded and unpainted.

"It just sat there," said Bud Roberts aloud, his

breath showing in the freezing room. "It just sat there doing nothing. Weird . . ."

But then things got even weirder. The next entry was dated seven days later, and it had the Mac returning to San Diego—returning with absolutely no indication that it had even left. The cargo it carried this time was off-loaded, but there was no indication of what that cargo had been, or exactly where the ship had gone to pick it up.

Then things returned to normal for the enormous cargo ship. It got its promised paint job, followed, as if a kind of bonus, by an engine overhaul and some cargo-hold reworking. Then she was off for another two years of refueling carriers in the Pacific.

Bud turned back to the page of strange comings and goings and noticed something he had not seen before. Where the Captain's name should have been was the set of abbreviations TDY—they meant that he was on temporary duty somewhere else. And in the space where the acting Commander should have been, Bud found only a blank space. He peered at it closely and decided that the name had been erased. Bud knew he needed to know that name and that meant he was going to have to go deeper into that dungeon. But first he was going to go find an overcoat.

thirteen ✈

WHEN THE INQUIRY RESUMED, ADMIRAL
Eric McKitrick was in the witness chair. Burgess was
as cool and collected as he had been earlier and, Harm
noted, was again working without notes. He didn't
really need them—McKitrick was aloof, lordly, almost disdainful, as if he was above the whole proceeding. Burgess was about to lead him through the
now very familiar events of the night on the Cats Paw
II, when Admiral Selden interrupted.

"Commander Rabb?"

Harm jumped to his feet. "Yes, sir?"

"May I ask where your client is?"

"I . . . I don't know, sir. I expect Major MacKenzie
and Captain Phillips any moment, sir."

At that moment the door opened and Mac walked

quickly into the room. Harm could tell in a glance that there was something wrong. He looked to Selden. "May I have a moment to confer with the Major?"

The Admiral grumbled and nodded; Harm took that as permission.

Mac leaned into his ear. "You're not going to believe this," she whispered. "You are *not* going to believe this."

"At this point, in this case, I would believe anything," Harm replied. "Lay it on me—but I'm betting it's not good news."

"It isn't—he's missing."

"Phillips? Phillips is missing. How do you mean, missing?"

"No one can find him. They can't find him anywhere."

Admiral Selden pounded his gavel. "Your client, Commander Rabb?"

"He seems to be missing, sir."

"May I suggest that you find him. I am ordering a recess. Commander Rabb, you have thirty minutes."

"Yes, sir. Thank you, sir."

It took ten minutes or so for Harm and Mac to put together a search party. They had twenty Marines at their disposal, plus the two of them, to search every corner of the vast vessel. If he didn't get Phillips back to the courtroom, there would almost surely be a contempt charge against him, but that was small potatoes—Harm was worried about something a lot darker. With the evidence mounting against him—capped by Conroy's damning account of the argument between Hawkes and Phillips—Harm couldn't help but feel that his worst fears had come true. Maybe the stress had gotten to be too much for Phillips and he had decided to take the easy way out.

Conroy was the key. Phillips had said Conroy was lying; Harm could put him on the stand and have him say this. But both he and Phillips knew that such a denial would do no good—it was Conroy's word against that of Phillips. Why would Conroy lie? And Phillips had every reason to. . . .

For a second, Harm cursed himself for not tracking down the man who had driven the cab that night—maybe he could have broken the tie—but there was no time for that now.

Harm had the Marines spread out all over the ship, each of them equipped with walkie-talkies that would beep only on the receivers that Harm and Mac were carrying—a sort of high-tech version of attorney—client privilege. One thing Harm wanted to avoid at all costs was news of the Captain's disappearance from spreading all over the ship—the last thing a ship headed for troubled waters needed was news of a panicky, possibly suicidal captain.

"I want this search done quickly and quietly," MacKenzie ordered the Lance Corporal in charge. "And anyone who opens his mouth is going to get two weeks in engineering."

Engineering was a nice way of saying working in the very bottom of the ship, in the foul bilges. They wouldn't see the sun for a full fourteen days.

"Sir," said the Lance Corporal, "Yes, sir!"

Harm and Mac made their way up to the Captain's

Quarters. It didn't take them more than a moment to find the note. It was taped to the green, shaded lamp on the desk. It was simple and to the point: "I love my kids and my wife very much," it read. "I did not kill my friend, but I have been forced to face the facts that there is some sort of conspiracy at work here; someone has decided that I did kill Allen and will have to take the fall for it. I will not go to prison for a crime I did not commit. I did nothing wrong. God Bless America."

They had both seen suicide notes before and they had long ago learned that the shorter the message, the more likely the writer would carry out his intention to commit suicide. The note was written in a clear, firm hand—another bad sign, a signal that Captain Phillips really had made up his mind to kill himself. Many suicide notes talked about conspiracies, which were usually the ravings of a deranged mind—but in this case. Harm and Mac were inclined to believe him.

No sooner had they read the note when Harm's radio began to beep. "Rabb," said Harmon.

It was the Lance Corporal of the Marine Guard. His voice was even, as if reporting in on something routine. "We've found him, sir . . ." the Marine said, "but you better get down here ASAP."

At the rear of the enormous aircraft carrier was a small balcony which served as a platform where repairs could be carried out on several small rear-projected antennas. It was located at mid-deck, meaning it was not far from the surface of the water. At the stern of the boat, the water churned up by the carrier's powerful propellers created a small storm on the surface of the placid sea. It was not uncommon for a sailor to take a final plunge off a carrier. The ship was a small city containing 5,000 people and, as in any group that large, there were bound to be some with emotional problems severe enough to take the ultimate dive.

If one plunged into the turbulent wake churned up by the ship, there was no chance of survival. And the closest one could get to that wake was this tiny service balcony. It was there that the Marines found Captain Phillips.

He was in full uniform, holding a small box that contained, Harm assumed, his medals. He was staring out at the sea as if mesmerized by the roiling white wake.

Three Marines were on hand. They were armed with a length of rope and a pair of handcuffs, ready to tackle and restrain Phillips if Harm or MacKenzie gave the order—but there was no guarantee that they could get to him before Phillips had vaulted the low barrier and dropped into the sea.

"Pull back," Harm said to the Marines. Then, leaving Mac at the open hatch, he walked out onto the balcony, stood next to Phillips, and followed the line of his gaze.

"Nice view," he said as calmly as possible.

Phillips managed to tear his eyes away from the wake. He looked over at Harm, smiled sadly, and nodded.

"It's funny," the Captain said. "Any ship I've served on, I've always found the best place to sit was up front. And when I got the chance, I'd spend as much time as I could up there, just watching the water in front of us. Wondering what it was going to be like when we got to where we were going. Wherever it was . . . I just couldn't wait to get there.''

A gust of wind blew across the service perch. Harm moved a step closer to Phillips.

''Now,'' the Captain continued, speaking slowly, deliberately, ''I stand here looking at where we've been.'' He shook his head as Harm inched a little closer. ''It's been a good life . . . until the last week, I suppose. I just never thought it was going to end this way.''

''Sir—''

''Conroy lied.''

''That's right. We'll prove it. And—''

''I know Steve Conroy. He lied because he was ordered to lie. And if he was ordered to lie, then something is going on. And someone has to take the fall for it. And someone has decided that that someone is me.''

''Look, I'll put Conroy on the stand and prove that he lied.''

Phillips half-smiled. ''In an hour?''

But Harm wasn't thinking about that. He had backed up a bit. ''What do you mean, something was going on?''

Phillip's shrugged. ''I don't know what it was. But you can bet it was something. Me, I just drove around in the Ugliest Ship in the Navy.''

Out of nowhere, Harm remembered a single, salient fact, something had seemed so important when he first heard it but which had been superseded by events. "Did you know that Allen Hawkes had a security review last month?"

"So?" said Phillips. "He was scheduled for one, probably. We all have 'em, you know."

"It was his second security review in two months."

Phillips shrugged, as if he had lost any interest in the case. Harm got the distinct feeling that he was determined to go over the side. He ran through his options in his mind. There was really only one: grab Phillips and hang on until the Marines could leap out and help him. But if he grabbed Phillips and he struggled, there was a good chance that they would both go over the side.

"Sir, I can still win this case," said Harmon Rabb desperately.

"No you can't. And I'd be careful if I were you, Commander. Because if they decide that you got too close to discovering whatever they were up to, you could meet with an accident, too."

It seemed hopeless then. It seemed like there was nothing left to say. No words that could convince Phillips that all was not lost, that there was still some small shred of hope.

Then he heard Mac's sweet voice ringing out above the roar of the waves. She sounded like the Angel of Mercy.

"Harm!" she called out. "Bud! We've finally heard from Bud!"

It seemed in that moment that everything just stood still. The wind stopped blowing, the sound of the turbulent water faded away. Even the melancholy on

Phillips's face seemed to melt a little, as if warmed by the joyful tone in Mac's voice.

Harm kept his eyes on Phillips as he inched his way back to the open hatchway. Mac was smiling broadly, a piece of paper in her hand.

"Here," she said, proffering it. "It's from Bud."

Harm took it and read it quickly. Then he looked up at her. Then he read it again. "Really?" he said. "Can this be true?"

"He's also faxed us half of the information in the entire Maritime Records Depository. It's inside. You'll have to take a look. It's amazing."

Harm looked back at Phillips, who was staring back at both of them. Harm walked over and handed the message to the Captain. "Here," he said. "I think this might interest you."

Phillips read the communiqué and suddenly his face brightened. "Good God!"

Harm grinned happily. "What do you say, Captain? Let's get back to court, shall we?"

Phillips thought about it for about a second, then he grabbed Harm's hand and shook it. "Aye, aye, sir," he said with a grin. "And you're the boss."

Fourteen ✈

FOR SOME REASON, THE INQUIRY ROOM
seemed a little bigger when Harm, Mac, and Phillips
entered, followed by a respectful group of Marines.
Selden looked at his watch when the little party entered.

"You were about thirty seconds away from being
found in contempt," he announced as they took their
places at the defense desk. "Now, if we could pro-
ceed. . . ."

Eric McKitrick took his place on the folding chair,
and once again Burgess took him through the events
of the evening. He had not been present at the cab
ride, had heard of no argument, and had returned to
Washington on the Cats Paw II. If anyone aboard the
yacht that night had not killed Hawkes, it was

McKitrick. His alibi was rock-hard. It seemed plain to Selden that this witness had added nothing to the proceedings and had been called merely because form required it.

"No further questions," said Burgess.

Selden looked over at Rabb, expecting that he would have no questions. After all, what could he possibly need to know from McKitrick?

"Any questions, Commander Rabb?" McKitrick was half out of his chair.

"Oh, yes, sir."

"You do?" Selden looked surprised. "Then be my guest."

Harm circled McKitrick for a moment before asking his first question. "Admiral McKitrick . . . You told me once that you deal in logic."

"That's true."

"Were you aware that Captain Hawkes was under scrutiny by the NIS? That he had not one, but two security reviews in less than a month?"

"I was aware of that, yes."

"And using that fact, what do you infer, logically?"

McKitrick thought for a moment. "I would infer that he had done something that the NIS wanted to know more about."

"Any idea what that might have been?"

McKitrick shook his head slowly. "I have no idea."

"But would you say he was in trouble?"

"Objection," said Burgess. "Speculation."

"We are dealing in logic, here, Admiral," Harm

countered. "I'm asking the Admiral to apply his powers to the question at hand."

"Call it what you want, Commander. It's still speculation. Sustained."

"I have no further questions," said Rabb with a shrug.

"Commander Burgess?" asked Selden. "Cross?"

"No, sir. The prosecution rests."

Selden looked at Harmon Rabb. "It's all yours now, Commander. Call your first witness."

"Thank you, sir. I call Captain Joseph Phillips."

There was a small gasp in the room. It was common practice to call the accused last, not first. "Are you sure?" Selden asked.

"Oh yes, sir."

Phillips sat down in the witness chair. "Captain Phillips, when you were Commander of the USS *Mackinac*, did you ever sail empty?"

Phillips smiled and shook his head. "Empty? Commander Rabb, the Mac never sailed unless it was filled to capacity."

"And what was that capacity?"

"44,808," said Phillips. "That's a number I know better than my kids' birthdays."

"Can you think of a reason *why* the *Mackinac* might sail with less than its allotted cargo?"

"No. It would defeat the purpose, the mission of the vessel," said Phillips. He looked hard at Conroy. "Despite what has been said about the Mac in this room, it had an essential mission, a very important role to play in Naval strategy. I was proud to command her and the crew was proud to serve on her."

Harm gave a signal to Mac. "Admiral, I would like to introduce into evidence the manifests of the USS *Mackinac* during the time that it was commanded by Captain Phillips."

Mac advanced and placed a stack of slimy faxes on the table in front of the judge. The judge and everyone else in the room looked puzzled.

"As you can see, the ship never sailed with anything less than a cargo weight of 44,808."

"Yes," said Selden slowly. "Very interesting." He did not look interested in the papers at all.

Harm turned back to Phillips. "Captain Phillips, who commanded the *Mackinac* in the years before you took over?"

"Captain Allen Hawkes," he said.

"No further questions," said Harm, walking briskly back to his table.

There was a moment of silence as the court, Selden, and Burgess tried to make sense of what they had just heard.

Selden blinked a couple of times, then looked at Burgess. "Do you have any questions for this witness, Commander?"

The prosecutor knew that he *should* ask some questions, and he had intended to hammer away at the drunkenness of the evening and the argument in the cab, but Harmon Rabb was plainly up to something, and Burgess had neither the slightest idea what it was nor how to counter it.

The prosecutor got to his feet slowly. "Captain Phillips . . ." he began, but the fire seemed to have gone out of him. "On the night in question, did you have a lot to drink?"

"This again," mumbled Selden.

"Yes," said Phillips.

"Did you have an argument with Captain Hawkes? In the cab, I mean?"

"No."

"*No?* But Colonel Conroy has testified that there was a vicious exchange between you and Captain Hawkes."

"I know."

"Are you suggesting that he lied?"

"He did lie," said Phillips evenly. "But I have no idea why he would do that."

"Neither do I," said Burgess. "But I do know why you might. You might lie about it to avoid indictment for murder. Is that not so?"

"I did not kill Allen Hawkes," said Phillips firmly.

"I suggest that you did. I suggest that in a fit of anger and your mind befuddled by alcohol, you got a gun, went to the Officer's Quarters at Newport News, and shot the man who not only insulted you, but who blocked your career advancement. Is that not so?"

"That is not so," said Phillips.

Burgess threw up his hands, as if he had been dealing with a recalcitrant child he had caught in a fib. "No further questions, sir."

Selden turned to Rabb. "Commander?"

"I would like to call Colonel Conroy to the stand, sir."

• • •

Conroy did not look happy at being recalled. Harm went right at him. "Colonel Conroy . . . where were you in April, 1989?"

The SEAL looked angry. "How the hell am I supposed to remember that? I would have to consult my notes, my diaries."

"That's okay sir," said Harm brightly, waving Mac forward with another set of faxes. "We checked for you." He turned to Selden. "Sir, I would like to enter in evidence the passenger manifest for the USS *Mackinac* for the dates in question. You will see quite clearly that then Major Conroy was aboard the ship during that period."

Mac laid the fax in front of him. Selden glanced at it. "Okay. That's where you were, Colonel."

"The *Mackinac* was traveling between Panama and San Diego," said Harm. "Three trips in three weeks. And each time it went out, it went out light, well below the maximum cargo weight as established by the testimony of Captain Phillips."

Mac had the appropriate faxes, and she laid them before the Admiral.

"Now, Colonel Conroy, would you have any idea *why* that might have been?" Rabb asked affably.

"I—"

Harmon Rabb held up his hand, like a cop stopping traffic. "Before you answer, let me ask you two more questions. When you were aboard the USS *Mackinac*, who was the commanding officer?"

"Allen Hawkes," "said Conroy.

"Now—the other question. Any idea why the Mac went out light on those trips to Panama?"

154

Conroy opened his mouth to answer, but again Harmon Rabb stopped him. "Just one thing, Admiral Selden. I wonder if the Mac actually did go out light? It's odd—it was traveling well below capacity, and yet it burned the same amount of fuel on those trips that it would have if it were carrying the 44,808 tons that we've all come to recognize. . . ."

Mac placed the appropriate fax in front of the judge. "How many more of these things do you have, young lady?" Selden grumbled.

"That's it, sir, I think."

Harmon Rabb beamed at Colonel Conroy. "*Now*, Colonel, tell us why you think the USS *Mackinac* went out light?"

Conroy was pale. "It wasn't light," he said softly. He looked over at McKitrick. McKitrick glared back.

"Oh? What was on the ship?"

"Weapons," said Conroy.

"Anything else?"

"Ammunition, uniforms, vehicles."

"And who were they for?" asked Rabb. "Were they for the use of U.S. Navy personnel?"

"No."

"Who were they for, sir?"

"That's classified," said Conroy.

"Classified or illegal, Colonel?"

McKitrick stood up. "Admiral Selden, as the senior intelligence officer here, I'm afraid that I have to ask that this line of questioning be stopped at this juncture. It could have bearings on national security."

"Sit down, Eric," growled Selden. "And don't be such a pompous ass." He turned to Conroy. "Colonel, I think you had better come clean.''

"Conroy!" McKitrick yelled. "You keep your mouth shut!"

WHAM! The gavel came down and everyone jumped about a foot. "You shut up, McKitrick. Lance Corporal!"

The Marine Lance Corporal went taut. "Sir!"

"Remove the Admiral, please."

"Yessir!"

"Ambrose," McKitrick yelled, "don't be a damn fool!"

"Lance Corporal, put the Admiral in irons and remove him to the brig."

"Yessir!"

It took a moment to hustle McKitrick out of the room. He did not go easily, demanding to be put in touch immediately with the Secretary of the Navy, the Joint Chiefs, and the President.

Once he was gone, Selden turned back to Conroy. "Now, Colonel . . . if you would be so kind as to tell us what you know."

"McKitrick and the rest of the spooks had decided to do an end run around Congress," said Conroy softly. "We were picking up where Iran-Contra had left off, bringing guns and material and advisors into Central America through Panama. The manifests were faked to hide the black cargo. And unlike other operations, damm it, we got away with it!''

Harm picked up the thread. "Until NIS somehow got word of it and started leaning on Hawkes. You were afraid that Hawkes was going to crack and tell him what had been on the Mac all those years ago."

Conroy nodded.

"So you killed him. Under orders from Admiral McKitrick."

Conroy nodded again.

"No further questions, Admiral."

The admission had left those in the Inquiry room stunned and silent. Even the constant roar of jet fighters being launched off the deck above them seemed to lessen in intensity. Selden looked at the other members of the board, conferred with them briefly in an undertone, and then banged the room back to order.

"It is the unanimous conclusion of this board that Admiral McKitrick and Colonel Conroy be returned to the United States of America to face charges of murder in the first degree." He looked over at Captain Phillips. "And to you, Captain, this court extends its apologies."

Phillips nodded and then bowed his head. Harm could tell that Phillips was offering up a silent prayer.

Selden checked his watch. It was 1130 hours and the *Eisenhower* was just thirty minutes away from her combat station. Once she was in place, the long-awaited counter strike by the Allies would begin.

"Captain Phillips," said Selden. "Now that you are free of this entanglement I suggest you take your place on the bridge of this ship and execute your duties."

Joseph Phillips looked up, straightened his shoulders, and then snapped off a sharp salute. "Yes, sir!"

Selden banged his gavel one last time. "Gentlemen . . . ma'am," he said with a nod toward Mac, "I

157

thank you for your participation. These proceedings are closed.''

Rabb slumped back in his seat. "Man . . . That was close.''

"It was," said Mac, "but you did a great job.''

"You did," said Burgess coming over, his hand extended. The two men shook. "That was some performance, Harm. I thought I had him nailed before I left Falls Church. When you started with all that manifest stuff, I had no idea where you were going with it. How did you do it?''

"Oh," said Mac. "We had a secret weapon.''

"Yeah?" said Burgess. "What is it?''

"George," said Harmon Rabb, "didn't you hear her? It's a *secret*.''

FIFTEEN ✈

THE USS EISENHOWER REACHED THE POINT known as Tango Charlie at exactly 1200 hours, right on schedule. The carrier and its attending fleet of twelve ships had managed to achieve something that would have appeared to have been impossible: it had crossed the North Atlantic, the Mediterranean, passed through the Suez Canal, and reached its contact point in sixty-six hours. Now Mac had a pretty good idea of what Harm meant when he said that the *Eisenhower* traveled at a top speed of "top-secret fast."

The Ike was the last piece of the puzzle—all allied forces were now in place. At last the task of dealing with the Qobos and the shipping trapped in the upper gulf could begin. The rest of the day was taken up with a conference between the Commanders of the major vessels in the area, a coordination of plans and strategy that Harm and Mac were not privy to. They were nothing more than passengers now, more in the way than anything else. Phillips had not had a mother to speak to them, had not even thanked them for saving his skin, but they knew he was busy—and they were sure he was grateful.

Late that night, Harm did pick up a little scrap of information. The operation was set to begin at 0700 hours the next day.

And that day dawned bright and sunny, with visibility practically unlimited, and with the seas calm in the fifty-mile security zone around the Straits of Hormuz. The quiet serenity of the scene was shattered at exactly 0700 hours when the first jet screamed down the *Eisenhower*'s flight path, launching over the clear seas. Thereafter, another jet launched every few seconds.

Of the five carriers in the region, the *Eisenhower* was slotted to play the dominant offensive role. While the other Navy and Air Force planes were assigned to cover the salvage and clearing operations in the Straits themselves, it would be the aircraft launched from the Ike that would hit the Qobos stronghold on the island, taking down the Silkworm launch sites before they had a chance to launch.

Should the Ike's pilots fail to attack and destroy the Silkworm launch sites, the salvage crews moving into the area would be sitting ducks. Much was riding on the shoulders of the Ike's fliers as in groups of twos and threes they were hurled off the mighty carrier's decks, literally shot into the blue skies by the incredible power of the steam-driven launch catapults.

And up on the bridge, watching it all, quietly giving orders, keeping track of the situation, was Captain Joe Phillips.

Despite the noise and excitement up on deck, Harm was in his cabin fast asleep. He had intended to get up and watch the launch but when his alarm sounded, he had just not been able to bring himself to get out of bed.

To say that he was exhausted was something of an understatement. From his trip to the USS *Tennessee* and his drop into hostile territory in Cuba to the events in the courtroom the day before, Harm had managed to snatch eight or nine hours of sleep in the last week. It was hard to believe, but just five days has passed since Bud Roberts had pulled him out of that MiG at Weekend Warriors. Five days since Admiral Chegwidden had put him on the Hawkes case. But somehow the fatigue hadn't bothered him all that much until the case had been resolved—then he began shutting down. The night before, he had been dozing over a plate of food in the ward room when Admiral Ambrose "Bull" Selden had strode up to him and patted him roughly on the shoulder. Harm had opened his eyes wide and jumped to his feet.

"That was a hell of a performance you put on in there today, Commander. I don't think I've ever seen anything quite like it."

"Thank you, sir," said Harmon. "I had a lot of help." He glanced over at Mac and smiled.

"By the looks of it, you had the help of Almighty

God and all His Saints and Angels, Commander,''
growled the Admiral.

"Well, not quite *all* of them, sir."

"Well, get some sleep now. You look like you're
about to fall facedown in the plate of chowder."

"Yes, sir."

So while Harmon Rabb planned to watch the beginning of this little war, he stayed in his bed, sound
asleep, while the storm clouds of the mission gathered
in the air above the *Eisenhower*. But Harm's peaceful
sleep would come to an abrupt end.

Delta Green Flight was the last group of aircraft to
launch off the *Eisenhower*. Delta Green was a typical
mission package: four F/A-18 Hornets, four F-14
Tomcat fighters, and one ancient EA-6 ECM communications jamming aircraft. This flight had a relatively simple task, an end run around the island and
the Silkworm launching sites. The idea for this back-
door approach was for the aircraft in Delta Green to
come out of the sun, batting clean up, looking for
anything missed in the first two strikes. It was a simple mission, but an extremely hazardous one—quite
possibly, the most dangerous mission that would be
flown off the Ike that morning—and no one on the
carrier or in Delta Green Flight had the slightest notion of the danger they were facing.

Advance recon photographs taken of the Island had
shown that the militant were armed with standard mobile anti-aircraft guns. It was assumed that the first
two pulverizing strikes would pulverize the tiny island, destroying the Silkworms and taking out the

hard to miss anti-aircraft guns. By the time Delta Green came over, there would be no anti-aircraft response. There was one problem—the recon photographs had failed to pick up one small piece of the militants' weaponry. Hidden as far from the Silkworm sites as you could go on the tiny island was a single Chinese built Silkworm surface-to-air missile (SAM), a mobile missile mounted on a launcher truck.

When the first allied strikes arrived over the island, the situation got desperate very quickly. The militant's little world was coming down around them, and the SAM was ordered to be brought up quickly. The SAM was turned on and began to move forward. Moments later, Delta Green flight arrived over the east end of the island.

The SAM was launched cold—that is, its acquisition radar had barely been turned on, thus there was nothing for the Delta Green flight to track. The launch officer fired the missile and it shot straight up in the air, directly up the hot pipe of the lead F/A-18. The pilot of the Hornet never saw the SAM coming.

It was only through the immense skills and a measure of good luck that the Hornet pilot was able to eject and bail before his aircraft disintegrated around him in mid-flight. His chute opened just as it was supposed to and the pilot—Lieutenant Charlie Chadwick—watched as the F-14s from his flight descended on the mobile SAM and vaporized it with their nose cannons.

"Nice shooting, guys!" Chadwick yelled. "But too Goddamn late!"

Chadwick's airplane corkscrewed into a hill about

halfway between the smoking ruins of the SAM and the place where the rest of the Ike's war planes were reducing the Silkworm sites to a heap of burning, melted metal.

Chadwick hit the ground hard, landing in a thick outgrowth of spine trees and juda bushes, dense brush covering the side of a steep dusty hill. Within seconds of landing, Chadwick had slipped out of his harness and gotten rid of his parachute, then activated the homing beacon built into his flight suit. Now it was time for evasive action.

The last his comrades saw of him, Chadwick was disappearing into the bush, but there were at least a hundred men, all armed, racing toward the hill, intent on capturing him. A downed American pilot, a hostage, would make a very nice bargaining chip.

Harm wasn't sure what he was dreaming about when he felt someone tugging at his arm. He awoke to see two large blue eyes looking down at him. It was Mac. She did not look happy.

"Only you could fall asleep during World War Three," she told him.

Harm sat up. "You heard the Admiral last night, who am I to disobey an order?" He lay down again. "Major MacKenzie, you are causing me to disobey an order from a superior."

"Harm . . ." Mac implored.

"Is that what they're calling it already," said Harm as he plumped his thin pillow. "World War Three?"

"Not yet," said Mac. "But something serious has happened. Something really serious. The officer in charge of the Air Group wants to meet you in the pilot-ready room right now.''

Now Harm was wide awake. He sat up. "The CAG? You sure?"

Mac nodded solemnly. "I'm sure," she replied.

"I'm not still dreaming, am I?"

"No," said Mac. "This is not a dream. This is not a drill."

Harm shook his head, as if to clear it. "In the pilot-ready room?" he asked, puzzled. "Why would the CAG want to meet me there?"

sixteen ✈

THERE WERE FOUR MEN WAITING IN THE
pilot-ready room—the ship's CAG; two officers from
ship's intelligence, including Kumagai; the man who
had welcomed them on board the Ike; and another
pilot. The four were gathered around a computer-
generated map.

As the supreme commander of the aircraft on the
Eisenhower, the CAG was the second most powerful
man on the ship, but he did not stand on ceremony.
He signaled Harm into the tight circle around the
map. "Get over here, Rabb. Take a look at this little
dilemma we got ourselves here."

Kumagai quickly brought Harm up to speed. "We
got a man down on the ass end of this island," he
said. "We are getting a strong signal from his homing

beacon, but the people in the air say he's surrounded by goofballs and it's only a matter of time before they find him. And we don't want that to happen."

The other intelligence officer picked up the story. "We know the militants aren't exactly supporters of the Geneva convention on POW," he said. "They could kill him. They could torture him. They could try and bargain their way out of getting blown back to the stone age."

"So," said the CAG, "obviously, we have to get that guy out of there immediately."

Harmon Rabb was wondering if they wanted him to go over there and sue the pants of the Qobos militants—because he could think of no reason why he should be privy to this information.

The CAG checked his watch. "We have a rescue chopper taking off right now," he said. "And it's gonna need three planes to ride shotgun for it."

Harm felt that he had to say something. "Excuse me, sir," he said, showing all the respect he could for this Olympian figure, "but what does this have to do with me? I'm a JAG officer."

The CAG looked up from the map. "You're a pilot too, right?"

Harm hesitated a moment. "Yes, I'm a pilot, but I was taken off flight duty because of night blindness—"

"Does it look like night out there to you, Commander?"

"No, sir. But—"

"No time for buts, Commander," the CAG said.

"I've got a man down and I'm a pilot short. Now, can you handle an F-14?"

"Yes, sir," said Harmon Rabb. He hoped he wasn't lying. He had plenty of flying time in F-14s, some in combat—but it had been such a long time since he had flown one of those complicated machines. "But it's been a while, sir."

The CAG slapped him hard on the back. "Hell, it's like riding a bicycle, Commander."

"Yes, sir," said Harm, a slightly sick feeling seeping into the pit of his stomach. No one had ever shot at him while he was riding a bicycle . . . but he didn't think this was the time or place to point out that fact.

"Good. Go get suited up and ready to launch in five minutes solid," the CAG said. "We've got the one extra plane on board and you've been elected to take it up."

Mac was standing on the windblown deck when Harm emerged from the pilot's hatchway. She had never seen him dressed in full battle regalia before and now the sight of him in a flight suit, helmet, pistol in his leg holster, gloves, boots and O-mask gave her chills—for two reasons. First, he looked very dashing. Second, she knew he was headed for terrible danger.

"My knight in shining armor," she yelled, but her voice was lost in the roar of engines and the powerful wind.

But Harm had seen her, waved, and snapped off a sharp salute. She waved and saluted back. She watched as he climbed into the massive fighter, the flight crew swarming over him, strapping him in. One of them went over a few things with Harm. He nodded and appeared to ask a few questions before the crewman gave him two taps on his helmet—the traditional gesture of good luck—then climbed down the access ladder. The canopy closed around Harm and his rear-seat officer, and Harm fired up the plane's mighty engines.

This was going to be a quick launch. The Search and Rescue helo had already departed, as had the Search mission EWO and the two covering F/A-18 Hornets. Harms's F-14 was wheeled over to the catapult and hooked up quickly. Much hand signaling followed, until all of the deck crew members were clear of the plane. Then Harm gave a salute to the launch officer and leaned his head back in the seat. There was a wild rush of steam, a scream of the Tomcat's huge twin engines—and two seconds later the plane was gone, hurled off the carrier edge of the carrier at 120 miles per hour.

Mac felt her breath catch in her throat. "Take care, Harm," she heard herself whispering as the F-14 quickly disappeared over the horizon. "Please . . ."

They rode in on afterburner the entire way, so it took but twelve minutes for Harm and the rest of the planes in the rescue package to reach the island. The island beneath them looked like something from a movie. There were dozens of airplanes bombing and strafing the island while dozens more were orbiting nearby. There were at least three squadrons of Air Force F-15s either going in or coming out, and twice as many Navy planes. Harm could spot a few British Tornadoes, a brace of French Jaguars and even German MiG-29s down there in the mix.

The island itself was totally engulfed in flames and smoke. From what he could make out, the island was bigger than he had expected it to be—long and finger-like on its west side, rugged and mountainous to the east. Miraculously, the soldiers on the ground had managed to bring an anti-aircraft battery into play and through the smoke and flame they were firing back at the planes above them. This was not the surgical strike, the neat little takeout that had been made so popular during the Gulf War, when CNN and the other TV networks had delighted in showing the film provided by the military of adroit, clean, one-missile-one-kill attacks. There was nothing clean about this attack; it was raw, brute force; quick, bloody, and devastating.

Harm and the planes in his flight began a wide turn out to the south and then jinked back north before turning west—the 240 degree turn took about three minutes as all three jets cooled down from after-burner.

They had caught up to and passed the SAR helo—a huge SH-53 Sea Stallion, armed to the teeth and hung with a heavy winch and recovery basket for picking up the downed airman. Harm did not envy the man. His own recent experience with this procedure had been harrowing enough, but he hadn't had to contend with a firestorm on the ground and a bunch of people shooting at him.

An F/A-18 from the initial Ike strike force had been circling the area where the pilot had gone down.

Harm heard the Hornet jock's voice crackle in his ear.

"Tango Green, Tango Green, I've already been down there and strafed a column of hostiles, but I didn't get 'em all and they are getting close to our guy. Next time I make a pass, I could put him right in the middle ·of the shitstorm. I'm running out of ammo and fuel is becoming a factor."

"Roger that," Harm replied. "I guess that makes us the cavalry. We'll take it from here."

"Fine with me," came the reply. "Our guy is at coordinates 555/6/W. Least, he was a minute ago."

"I got it," Harm replied. "See you back on the Ike."

"Roger," the Hornet replied. He rolled over, righted himself, then turned back toward the USS *Eisenhower*.

Harm now took his aircraft down to a stomping altitude of 8,500 feet and let the Hornets and the chopper do the stuff. His job was to watch out for any enemy fighters that might interfere with the SAR operation, or to spot any more SAM or AA sites that might shoot up at the rescuers.

He waited for the SAR helo to go into its hover. Then he heard that one of the Hornet pilots had picked up a good beacon signal from the pilot below. That piece of information was followed immediately by bad news from the helo pilot.

"There are hostiles—a lot of them on the far side of the hill," he said. "They're using our position to find our guy."

"Roger," said one of the Hornet pilots. "I'll take care of them." Harm saw the Hornet peel off and dive on this small army of men. The nose cannon opened up, slashing through the ranks, cutting down more than half and scattering the rest.

But now a new threat arose. To the south Harm could see a small column of armored trucks accompanied by at least two tanks heading up fast toward the back of the hill. The hill was under attack from three sides now. The first Hornet pilot was still dealing with the soldiers climbing the north face. The second Hornet was busy communicating with the downed pilot and protecting the SH-53. That left only Harm to deal with the mobile threat.

But there was a slight problem. The F-14 was not really built for ground attack. It was a pure fighter— an aircraft specifically designed to shoot down other aircraft. But Harm didn't have time to be concerned with the niceties of aircraft design just at the moment. There was a serious threat approaching the downed pilot—a threat serious enough to take down the chopper as well.

There was a big nose cannon on the Tomcat and a full tank of ammo. More than enough to improvise with. Harm had no idea who his rear seater was—his GIB—but he hoped that he was a good sport.

"Hang on back there," Harm yelled, then he put the Tomcat into a screaming dive.

The soldiers in the armored column saw him coming and did a foolish thing—they stopped dead on the dusty track. All six vehicles kicked up clouds of fine sand with the simultaneous screeching of the brakes. Harm was down to a hundred feet and still dropping when he saw the orange flashes of fire popping out of this cloud of dust.

Harm started wigging and wagging as his rear seater began yelling out threat locations. Harm knew that this close to the ground the Tomcat could be a little wild, tough to handle—the plane was really too fast for its own good. Still, he bore down and at 500 yards out he opened up with the F-14's big cannon. The entire airplane began to rattle and shake. They were so low and going so screamingly fast, with the cannon blasting rapid fire, probably violating at least a half a dozen laws of aerodynamics, Harm thought—but they were still in the air and laying down fire, and that was all that mattered at the moment.

Harm followed the streaks of his cannon fire as they pierced the cloud of dust, and several seconds later saw fire blow up through the murky air. These had to be secondary explosions—which meant he had hit something down there. He finally pulled up and looped around. By this time the cloud of dust had blown away, Harm could see that he had knocked out two of the armored trucks.

"Great shooting!" yelled his rear seater.

"Dumb luck," Harm shouted back. Actually, it had been blind luck—literally. But there were still four more vehicles down there intact and now they were closing in on the position of the downed pilot.

Harm looped back around and dove again. Once again the smoke and dust closed his vision down to zero, so he simply aimed the nose of the jet at the smudge, yanked the cannon lever, and let fly. He was streaking in as close to the deck as possible—down near 150 feet, hoping that if the slugs from the cannon didn't scatter the enemy, the wild screech of his engines would.

He looped around again and once more the dust had blown away. Once again he had received more than his fair share of luck. Two more vehicles—one of the tanks—were flaming wrecks. But this left two more—the last two. One more loop and shoot, Harm told himself, and prayed his luck would hold. This time he went straight into the firestorm, opened up the cannon again, and felt the plane shudder as if it were trying to shake him out of it. Then suddenly there was silence—or a sort of silence. The cannon was not firing anymore—it had run dry—and his ears were filled with the scream of his engines alone.

"Damn it!" Harm yelled. This called for one more loop—unarmed. He turned the plane over and lost altitude, coming down fast—but all he could see was a lot of damn smoke. Had he killed the last tank and truck, or would they get to the downed pilot? He dove again and rode through the smoke, zooming in so fast that he sucked a lot of the noxious clouds along with him in his wake. The area beneath them cleared.

It was the backseater who yelped first. "Damn, man that's some shooting!" The man was yelling into his headset so loud that Harm felt his ears stinging. "Got 'em all, buddy. Got 'em all."

Somehow Harm had clipped the last two vehicles with the last few shells in his gun. Now they lay smoldering and aflame not fifty yards from where the downed pilot was being lifted up by the helo's winch.

"When's the last time you were out on the range?" the RIO yelled. "Looks like you were flying Top Gun ground school 'bout a week ago."

Harm had to smile when he heard that. "Would you believe it's been more than five years?"

But the RIO wasn't listening. He was too wrapped up in watching the successful pilot pick-up down below. Suddenly Harm's headphones were filled with the excited voice of the RIO. "Okay. We got him! Let's get the hell out of here!"

At the same time one of the Hornet pilots was yelling, "Go! Go! Go!"

Harm did not need any more prompting. He put the Tomcat on his tail and gave it the full boot. This forced hundreds of gallons of raw fuel to be dumped onto the hot end of his engine, and the afterburner kicked in. Suddenly they were rocketing through the sky at twice the speed of a bullet.

Below and behind them, the island was burning. The Silkworm sites had been devastated and so had the cadres of soldiers. The island looked the way the surface of the moon would look like if someone had set it on fire. What made it all better was the report that flashed through their headphones: that all planes were returning safely to their various bases and already Teheran was calling for a peaceful solution to the problem.

Harm smirked at this.

Problem? What problem, he thought as he caught one last look at the cratered island. The U.S. Navy and Air Force, the French and the British, had just taken care of the problem. And all in less than ten minutes.

Harm banged down on the Ike fewer than thirty minutes later. All of the strike fighters had returned by this time and the rescue chopper was coming in for a landing.

Harm's plane was surrounded by a small gang of deckhands as soon as his aircraft was yanked to a halt by the arresting cable. Word of his unorthodox attack on the Qobos column had already reached the Ike. The deck crew appeared to be staring up at him with something like awe. Suddenly Harm felt self-conscious.

He popped the canopy, unbuckled himself, and climbed out of the cockpit. As he came down the access steps, he realized that the adulation was not directed at him, but at his plane. He joined the crowd, wondering what all the fuss was about.

"Damn!" said one of the ground crewmen. "Beats me how this thing still flew all the way home."

Harm soon found out. The bottom of the F-14 was absolutely riddled with bullet holes, dozens of them. Harm's breath caught in his throat—some of the rounds had hit mere inches away from critical parts of the airplane: the electrical boxes, the weapons boxes, even the fuel tanks. It was a wonder that the jet had pulled through. Harm shivered for a moment, thinking that he and his RIO could be back on that island, waiting for rescue just like the guy they had just picked up.

"Really like showing off, don't you, Commander?"

Harm turned. Mac was standing there beaming at him. At that moment she looked even more beautiful than usual. Then she shocked him by actually enveloping him in a tight hug. It lasted one second, two seconds—maybe even three. Harm enjoyed every heartbeat of it.

"Some day I'll tell you what really happened," he said, looking back at the pock-marked fuselage.

"I'm not sure I want to know," she replied.

epilogue ✈

THE WEATHER WAS PERFECT FOR SAILING.
The sea was calm, or as calm as the Mediterranean
could be as winter came on. The air was warm but
not stifling. The sun sparkled on the water and on the
gleaming jets lined up on the deck of the *Ike*. It was
as if Nature herself was saying to the crew: thanks
for a job well done.

The carrier's operations went on as usual. Planes
were being launched, planes were coming in, the famous dance of the desk proceeding unhindered—
though there was a palpable sense of relief among the
crew. They had faced the devil and defeated him—
everyone had come home safe—and the world was a
little safer, too.

A C-2C Greyhound out of Naples, Italy, slammed

down on the deck with the usual scream and a bang. The twin props of the plane kicked up a storm of wind and spray, sending a cool mist wafting across the deck. Unlike most arriving aircraft, this plane would not be staying long. It was here to pick up two passengers, then it would depart, returning to Naples where the passengers would be placed on a C-5 and carried across the Atlantic. They would reach Newport News by nightfall.

The side door of the island opened and the pair were led out. Conroy and McKitrick, clad only in sailors' utilities, their feet and hands shackled, made their slow walk to the C-2C. Conroy's cheeks burned with humiliation and he kept his eyes down; McKitrick, on the other hand, walked erect and proud.

Harm and Mac were standing by on the deck awaiting the banging in of their own air taxi. It would carry them to the U.S. Naval Air Station at Olbia to await transport back to the U.S. If they got in a couple of days on Sardinia's beautiful beaches before the right plane showed up . . . well, as Harm said: "You go where the Navy sends you. . . ."

As the pair of accused murderers was led out under Marine guard, McKitrick whispered something to the Sergeant in charge. The guard nodded—somewhat reluctantly—and led McKitrick over to Harm and Mac. He stopped in front of them and looked them over, as if really seeing them for the first time. The wind blew his gray hair every which way and, for the first time since either had laid eyes on the spook, McKitrick looked unkempt, small, and rather ordinary.

"I feel that I must congratulate you two," he said.

"And as odd as it might sound, you were nothing less than brilliant. I cannot claim to be happy with the outcome, of course, and in due time this mess will be resolved and *I* at least will be cleared of these ridiculous charges."

Harm just nodded. If he couldn't get Phillips to take the fall, he'd try and get Conroy to draw the short end of the stick. McKitrick didn't care who went down for his crimes, as long as it wasn't him.

"What is it you want, exactly?" Harm asked, his voice full of disgust. "Your transport is waiting."

"Let it wait," McKitrick snapped. "We have a long road ahead of us, Conroy and I," he said firmly. "I envision a long trial."

"Do you think so?" said Harm. "I think it will be brief."

McKitrick nodded. "Be that as it may," he said, "I would like you to consider something."

"And what is that?" Mac asked.

"I think you two are the best in the business," McKitrick said. "And I could use your help. I would like you to defend me. Will you consider it?"

Harm and Mac exchanged a quick glance, and they knew their decision in an instant.

Harm spoke for both of them. "Forget it," he said.